GOLF WIDOWS REVENGE

C

Dedic

John 'O', F

CW01072680

I would like to thank everyone who helped and supported me during the writing of Golf Widows Revenge, especially my dear travelling companion Dott Whittle. My special thanks, however, must go to Graham Dixon without whom none of this would have been put into print – thanks Graham.

The events, people and places within this story are fictitious (honest) similarities to any person living or dead are coincidental.

Golf Widows Revenge was conceived many years ago in a fit of utter boredom. The introduction was written just as an amusing diversion to read to some of my friends who were in a similar state of frustrated boredom. The friends all found it amusing and suggested all kinds of revenge, mostly of a sensual or sexual nature!

I put the paper away and forgot about it for quite a few years. One day while sorting through a file I found it again, and reread it. I was still enduring the long evenings and tedious weekends of boredom whilst hubby played golf, so I decided to take up my pen again and continue where I had left off years before. I would need to research how these revenges would take place. The what, where, when and how of it was quite fruitfully discussed around the coffee tables of many friends, and later as I began to write, around the swimming pool in Tenerife. It was written with a fertile and vivid imagination and with much laughter.

I must be honest, not one ounce of truth was in the writing, just a great deal of creative wishful thinking. I long to be Ella or Tanya, or any of the ladies who try to take life by the balls and give it a good squeeze; I guess my way is to write about it. I'm far too old to flaunt it, but the youthful memories linger on. The desire to be young, sexually attractive and lively was always at the top of the list of discussions with my fellow researchers, especially my daughter Joanna who gave me some of the more youthful phrases and sexual nomenclatures. I am indebted to her for Ella's story and her rather glamorous and feisty image.

I do love Italian sculptures and have spent happy hours admiring those mentioned in my story, especially Donatello's David. That beloved little statue led me to endless discussions about the erotic nature of art and Italian art in particular.

My daughters have given me a joy in art, language, wine and food; they have given me several ideas, which have found their way into my story. I thank them most sincerely and hope that they are not too shocked at their mother's wildest fantasies. I have enjoyed immersing myself in this tale of womanly revenge and thinking of the motto while the cats away the mice will play, I've written while the golfers away see what the ladies might play.

GOLF WIDOWS REVENGE

Copyright Gilly Flower 2011
ISBN 9781475031607

GOLF WIDOWS REVENGE.

Chapter One

The Reason.

The little black estate car pulled crisply up outside the house. The door opened and Julia sprang gingerly out, jumped the small brick wall and ran up the path. She tapped lightly on the glass door and opened it. Tanya smiled as she looked up from the mountain of ironing.

"Well what time did they promise to be back today?" Julia asked with the sound of resigned sarcasm that conveyed she already knew the answer. Tanya plonked the iron down heavily with a sigh "Mark said three o clock but we know that means at least six; do you want a coffee?"

Julia sat down in a careless manner; she was casually dressed in Armani jeans and a pink Firenze silk shirt. Her hair was cropped short and dyed a baby blond. She wore little or no make-up, but her figure and youthful countenance belied the fact that she was on the doorstep of fifty. Tanya too was approaching that dreaded age and she also belied the fact.

She had eyes that revealed her wicked sense of humour and looks that had turned many a man's head in the past. Both women sat round the table waiting for the kettle to boil, suddenly Tanya slapped her hand down hard, "Sod it!" she said "let`s get out the Rhubarb wine…To hell with housework, money, Golf and men…and God bless home-made wine the solace of all those who require something more out of life than utter boredom!" Both women burst out laughing.

The wine was delicious and very heady, it had not been allowed to mature, but then so hadn`t many a bottle, especially on long Saturdays and Sundays. This little scene was regularly enacted by the two, who suppressed their anger and boredom and went on stoically week in week out…year in year out, being the little women who worked from Monday to Friday and then crammed the housework into the weekend, while their husbands (God bless them!)… played golf.

"You know Tanya I can`t think of anything more I`d rather do than wash the entire contents of three Alibaba baskets of men's clothes, Oh! No! I tell a lie…..I just adore ironing them!" Julia sipped her wine as she dropped these sarcastic little gems and Tanya eager to join in the irony exclaimed between large slurps of Rhubarb wine "Oh! But don`t you   just revel in the shear bliss of shopping at Asda? It's the highlight of my week to see if I can make £66.50 do what £106.50 should do." They subsided into giggles as the kettle began to scream.

Tanya got up switched the kettle off and poured out some more wine." Let's drink it in the conservatory, I can't bear to look at this heap of ironing any more", she said, averting her eyes from the impossible pile; Julia rose patted Tanya on the shoulder and said "You know, you shouldn't have made friends with a deviant devil like me…just think if I hadn't opened your eyes to the wider possibilities in life you'd really enjoy doing all these wonderful wifely duties!"

The regular ritual began again, as the two of them lounged in the warm conservatory; sipping wine with the sun warming them as they slipped into a world of fantasy, imagining events and situations of wider possibilities in life that they had not had but longed for. As the winter sun and the wine penetrated into them they sat in the warmth and dreamed.

They had both married young and had had children who were now grown up, and as always, away from them. Their lives were no longer child centred and they were too intelligent to find fulfilment in the humdrum existence of housework. They were too old however to become high powered career women and besides too many employers viewed married women as working only for: pin-money" to take them seriously. As for their husbands, well, these were men of yesteryear; handsome, yes, but as far as understanding their wives restless unease, this was just impossible for them. They thought women should be content in the home and enjoy doing things that women do. Mark and James accepted the fact that their wives worked' Julia as a part-time craft teacher at an Adult education centre and Tanya; well she had something to do with insurance. God knows didn't most wives have to work now to make ends meet, but, the men were the real bread winners, they did the proper jobs! So was it any wonder that frustration, boredom and anger were simmering gently in the breasts of these two suburban housewives, and golf was to be the catalyst that sparked the seeds of discontent and revenge.

It was growing quite late and the sun was edging its way down the skyline when Tanya woke from her reverie…"God what time is it Julia? The girls will be back and I promised them tea …Dam!" Julia looked at her watch and a cool anger crept over her, it was seven thirty and James had been away since seven that morning. She turned to Tanya and said quietly "It' seven thirty, I'd best be going just in case his Lordship deems to return, I'll ring you later bye!"

Julia returned to an empty house and sat in icy silence waiting. As the minutes ticked by her anger became tempered with a sweet desire for revenge .At 9 o clock she rang Tanya who was of course in exactly the same situation and mood." Hi! Tanya, are they there? No their not of course, how silly of me to ask, well come down and we'll wait together and pour our double venom upon them, when they do finally return."

Tanya came down and they waited and waited until just as the ten o clock news started, the sound of a car pulling into the drive was heard. Then the sound of suppressed giggles and whispers announced the imminent arrival of the prodigal golfers.

Tanya turned to Julia said flatly "They're back!" Julia was about to answer when the door was rudely flung open and the two errant golfers entered, jubilant with success; they had won their place into the next round. There followed a blow by blow account of the masterful strokes that these two supreme players had produced to secure their deserved place in the competition. Julia and Tanya sat in stony silence, but the men were oblivious to this as they sprawled languidly on their easy chairs. Flushed with whisky and success Mark turned to Tanya, smiled through a haze of joy and said "Had a good day, honey?" James too sat bathed in success and whisky he smiled and slipped lower into his chair, he slurred his words slowly as he inquired "Well what do you know love?" He was quite incapable of comprehending any answer, and as he and Mark slipped gently into subconsiousness, his last words were "Just resting my eyes love just resting my eyes."

"That's it!" said Tanya "I'm not putting up with this any longer!" this was said determinedly "this time, I mean it, I am going to enjoy myself, and bugger the consequences!" suddenly all the anger, frustration and pent up boredom exploded in Tanya's exaltations and expressions of escape.

Julia looked across at the two sleeping husbands and with a detachment that shocked her she replied to Tanya "We've said that before, but this time let's make a pact. These two don't give a damn about us, they've got it right, care about yourself, enjoy yourself at all cost so we'll do the same. All it needs Tanya is a plan, now what are we going to do when they next play golf?"

"I don't know about you but I'm starving, I was waiting to eat my tea with it (Tanya nodded her head towards Mark) but it doesn't seem to want any food or anything else for that matter. I know lets discuss the plan over a glass of wine and a pizza. There's that new Italian restaurant that stays open extremely late." Julia brightened visibly "Yes and we can chat up the waiters and boast our morale at the same time!"

7

The two women picked up their handbags and with a look of withering distaste towards their husbands, they walked out of the room and shut the door firmly but quietly behind them, and the men slept on!

Chapter Two.

Italy Tempts and Beckons.

The adrenalin pulsed through their veins as they sat in the car. Like two escaped prisoners eager to quit their jail but unsure of freedom and its' traps. They, for a few moments daren't proceed. Each seemed to breathe deeply as if they were about to attempt some major physical task, then they looked at each other and grinned broadly. Eyes sparkling and hearts thumping Julia triumphantly said "Right! Off in to the breach with us dear friend and to hell with the consequences!"

She drove quickly along the narrow roads, Tanya sat nervously by her side, already doubts creeping into her mind; this was wrong, she was a wife, a mother with responsibilities, not a free agent, how could she be doing this? But the little devil on her shoulder justified what she was about to embark on with the plausible explanation that Mark needed a lesson, one that he wouldn't forget for a long time. Besides she was depressed and aggrieved she needed some pleasure in life and she desperately wanted to be admired again as she had been when she was young and single.

By the time the little black Audi turned into Penguino's she had suppressed her conscience and was rearing to go. Julia switched off the engine, opened the door and stepped out as if this was a most natural occasion, she walked towards the restaurant, turned to Tanya and said "come on, don't forget to lock the door." Tanya knew that this air of bravado was a show and that deep down her friends hurt was very real. Julia was a little like a crab, hard shell on the outside but soft and tender inside, and for all her sarcasm and bravado, this was definitely a big leap out of boredom and neglect into …God knows what!

They pushed the double doors of Penguinos open; and the seductively inviting warmth and enticing smell of Italy rushed forward to greet them; for a moment they basked in the heady aroma, breathing in this erotic and sensuous mixture of wine and culinary delights.

A voice of pure liquid gold said "Well hello ladies!…Come in come in!" Julia and Tanya opened their eyes wide and gazed longingly for there just in the rosy warmth leaning behind a sparkling bar was …The most gorgeous Buonarroti David look alike you could ever see. The man was the spit of Michelangelo's David, perhaps older and greyer and only a mere six foot…but oh! The head and the hair and the sexy heavy eyes were a steal for that magnificent statue. Julia sighed a long sigh "Oh! Look at those lips, that perfect cupids bow and the eye brows very heavy, and one lifted in expectant anticipation." He smiled … the beckoning smile of a licentious Romeo. "Antonio Ullivari, at your service, how can I help you ladies?" He bowed slightly and then leaned forward over the bar his hand outstretched. Next to him stood a huge Sicilian bandit of a man, a large chested giant of a man with a short curly blue-black beard and a grin that melted butter. He laughed a gurgling belly laugh as he came forward, engulfing the girls in his big arms, wrapping one around each waist. "Vittorio Tartaglioni, ladies I will personally make sure Antonio give you the best of everything and I mean everything!" and the belly laugh came again, it was somehow very seductive and suggestive at the same time, and yes, it was really very, very inviting.

"Oh! Are we to late to eat?" asked Julia in a gasping whisper. Tanya turned towards Vittorio and tilted her head coquettishly "well we'd quite like a drink if we may?" and Vittorio responded "for you darling, we have the king of kings drink… come on Antonio –the Borolo Reservee get it out for the ladies!" Antonio lifted a large yet peculiar shaped bottle from behind the bar and poured the dark claret coloured wine into two large goblets. He handed one to Julia caressing the tips of her fingers saying "This wine is so deliciously perfect and full of body, that at one time in history it was reserved for kings and popes only… so sip it gently, slowly and allow its lusty body and ripe flavour to caress your tongue and throat!" Vittorio handed the other goblet to Tanya, squeezing her waist with his arm he murmured "Oh! Yes it was also considered the wine of Aphrodite…the juice of erotic and ecstatic love making! So *in vino veritas mia Cara*…I trust you will love this wine! Now darling tell me your name, so I can whisper it in my sleep! For surely; Aphrodite has sent you to me!" Tanya and Julia took a long draft of the deep dark wine! Oh! Yes it was very definitely a lush, lusty, full bodied and heady wine. "Mmm!" said Julia "I do adore Italian wine, culture, art, opera, furniture, food in fact everything to do with Italy it's so…so…" "Sensuous, sexy, erotic and tactile?" suggested Vittorio seductively. Antonio asked seriously "How come you like Italy so much and what do I call you?" Julia smiled gently; she was warming to this beautiful Michelangelo David look alike." I've always loved the Italian Renaissance, since I was at Art College, and the names Julia, really Juliet but no one calls me that."

"Oh! Juliet my Juliet, for that is what you are, I give you an evening of Italian culture, I will immerse you in wine and *Gamberoni Provinciale*, the food of love! And I will be your Italian culinary taste master teaching you to eat it the Italian way!"

Vittorio looked at Tanya smiled lovingly and pulled her even closer to his large chest; he looked deep into her eyes and gave her a wicked wink. "You sit next to me in that cosy corner, and I will immerse you in much more than *Gamberoni mia Cara!*" Tanya smiled up at him and looked languidly through her long dark lashes "The names Tanya, they call me hard hearted Tanya" and she laughed as Vittorio took her hand and led her into the dark recess of the restaurant. Antonio called "Vinni, two very large plates of *Gamberoni Provinciale* and another *Barolo*! And put the *Bollinger* on ice…you can leave us then…I'll close up."

11

Chapter Three

How to Eat Gamberoni and Much Much More.

Tanya and Julia sat down in the shaded alcove of the restaurant; the table was a large rectangular white marble one with carved marble pillars supporting it. It was heavy, cool and majestic to look at, Vittorio stroked it lovingly. "Beautiful, beautiful Caspian marble, smooth as velvet, cool, yet it warms to the touch of a lovers body, "you like it?" Tanya touched the marble stroking it "It's absolutely gorgeous; how I'd love to pose as Aphrodite sleeping on it as well!" She said this in jest as she was really enjoying this outrageous flirtatious teasing. Vittorio Tartaglioni was no match for her wit and love of the suggestive double entendre. "Be careful Mia Cara! You don't realise what I do for a living. I Vittorio Tartaglioni, own a quarry, a marble quarry near Firenze. The marble you are touching and stroking so fondly is marble I quarried and I carved especially for my friend Antonio Ullivari for his fine restaurant in England – I'm here to see how well it fits in with the décor and the customers, I might just keep you to your pose! A little later on!"

Julia sat opposite Antonio his eyes were blazing as he stared at her intently. He looked at her over the rim of his drink of Barolo, and smiled a very satisfied smile. He really liked the look of this mature attractive woman, even though she was wearing a wedding ring. At fifty three years of age and his own marriage on the rocks, he wanted, no, he craved and desired a little romance, and if this lady was seeking solace and a little comfort, well he was just the man to give it.

The *Gamberoni Provinciale* came, twelve very large and very spicy, red, king prawns, covered in a divine sauce of finely chopped Neapolitan tomatoes, crushed garlic, a liberal sprinkling of herbs, a few shallots, a dash of Chianti and just the tiniest hint of chilli. They had lain on this bed of sauce, until the juice had permeated the skin and now after a short hot blast in that Italian pizza oven, they were lovingly laid on a bed of pure white al dente rice, with just a few capers for company. They looked and smelt mouth-wateringly delicious. Julia positively drooled at them. She was just about to lift two onto her plate with a little rice when Antonio held his hand up, and pursed his lips and shook his head.

"No wait, Juliet darling, this dish is one of Italy's most romantic and seductive feasts, it must be very slowly enjoyed and with all the senses." His voice was whisperingly, husky; he leaned over the table and held her hand. "First, you must enjoy with the eyes, see how plump, fleshy and yet stiff these fine bright red Gamberoni are and how their heads all moist and juicy, juicy waiting to be licked and sucked." Julia's mouth opened slightly as she gasped at his seductive description. "That's right Cara! Open your mouth just a little. "He reached over , breathing heavily, he was very slowly moistening his own lushes lips, and as he did so he placed his right index finger on her lower lip pulling it very gently down ,and with his left hand… he held a large fleshy *Gamberoni* between his thumb and forefinger, "and now my darling it is time to slowly, very slowly, slip this hot and juicy head deep, deep into your mouth," he sighed heavily and looked into Julia's half-closed eyes. "Now! Suck my darling, a long slow suck and roll your tongue around the juicy head. "Julia took very deep breaths through her nostrils as she sucked the rich juice; she let it trickle down her throat. Antonio slowly pulled the head back and held it on her lips for a moment, and Julia gently licked the slightly salty sauce off the head. "Delicious" she whispered. Antonio looked at her with such dark longing eyes, and then he leaned even further forward and said in a velvet husky voice, whisperingly seductive in Italian "*Ti voglio, ti voglio penetrare fino al cuore con la mia freccia di Cupid!*" Julia was spell bound, she couldn't move, she felt on fire, her whole body was tingling with excitement and anticipation, all she could do was sigh, gasp and heave her breasts, while Antonio pulled back the head and peeled the king prawn, he gave it to her lovingly.

Vittorio and Tanya sat and watched transfixed with admiration. Tanya gazed into Vittorio's face and said "Gosh! It shouldn't be allowed but it sounds ever so erotic! What's he said? What's he said? Come on Vittorio you've got to tell me!"

Vittorio was full of admiration for his old friend Antonio. He was really getting over the break-up of his marriage, and how! Vittorio laughed and told Tanya "I can't possibly say that out loud, come here" and he held her head close to his lips and whispered sensuously in her ear "I need you! I want to shoot my cupids arrow deep into your very core." With that Vittorio thrust his tongue in her ear laughed his sexy voluptuous laugh. Tanya gasped and gave a spluttered laugh; she was really enjoying this evening's revenge, and she was dangerously flirting with a true spirit of abandon, she hadn't had as much fun in years!

"Now , Tanya, I must give you Gamberoni as Antonio gave his Julia, so close your eyes, and head back, and part your pretty lips for my juicy Gamberoni! " Vittorio was enjoying himself as well and entering into this game of suggestive *amore* with true Italian style. He had been a womanizer for years, and he loved women, especially those who played hard to get; it made the chase so much more exciting and infinitely more enjoyable.

He took the largest king prawn and rubbed it along her bottom lip, and very slowly he began to press it into her mouth and on to her moist pink tongue, and very slowly Tanya placed her beautiful pearly teeth round the neck of the Gamberoni. With a sharp snap she bit the head clean off, dropping it onto Vittorio's hand. She exploded with laughter as she saw Vittorio's astonished expression. "Mm-m Vittorio haven't you heard how the female Praying Mantis mates with the male. He mounts her only the once, and after a very slow

14

but frenzied copulation, she grips him lovingly round the neck and snaps his head clean off! You know the female of the species is far more deadly than the male. Now, darling feed me! Feed me!"

"Wow! This woman is magnificent, she's sublime, she's one in a million, and I've got to have more of her!" Vittorio was saying this out loud as he prepared more Gamberoni to eat, he laughed as he passed the plate to Tanya and she greedily ate mouthful after mouthful of this aphrodisiac feast.

Vittorio took a spoon and scooped a few mouthfuls also; in fact, they were racing to finish the dish. Who would have the most prawns? And who would have the last bite?

The soft lighting bathed the room in a blushing glow, the marble table glistened in the subtle light, Julia and Tanya felt warm, satisfied and dreamy. Yes, this was much better than Rhubarb wine and the company couldn't be more attentive and obliging. Their senses had truly been awakened, sight, touch, taste, smell and now the sound of Pavarotti singing sublimely drifted from somewhere in the distance.

"I've not felt this contented in years, it's as if I've found my paradise," Julia smiled and hummed the melody as Tanya sipped her wine. "Yes, but I suppose all good things must come to an end, it's getting late and we have to be getting back." Tanya said this in a small sad voice; she had really enjoyed this evening.

Vittorio grasped her round the waist and pulled her really close to his mountain of a chest. "I'm not letting you go yet Cara; your senses are not yet truly awakened. Come both of you, Antonio and I have something very beautiful to look at and to feel. Antonio; can we show them?" Antonio bowed and nodded his head and smiled a slow dreamy smile "I think these ladies deserve the best of Italy. Behind these doors the very best of Italy is being lovingly put together by my good friend Vittorio and me … We've been collecting, buying, saving and loving these things for years. Come! Come I give you my true love." He held his arms out and sang softly in Italian *"Waken Il mio – che di sensi waken il mio amore!"* Antonio and Julia went through the large ornate black and gold double doors, Vittorio and Tanya followed, into a dark heavily scented and cool room.

Chapter Four

Italian Art and Tuscan Marble Inspire a Plan.

Antonio turned on the light in the centre of the high ceiling. There hung the most exquisite crystal chandelier, it was heavy and ornate, and the crystals hung like huge dew drops off an enormous spider's web. It threw out golden gleaming rays of light that revealed a large sumptuous room with many alcoves and in each alcove there stood beautiful marble statues holding torches that were alight. It was like walking into an old Renaissance room in some Medici Palace. In each alcove and recess hung tapestries or paintings or exquisitely carved works of art. Most of the paintings were of naked women, beautiful, full bodied nymphs laughing or smiling out of the gilt frames. In one alcove there stood a miniature replica of Michelangelo's David it was magnificent.

Antonio Ullivari turned to Julia and bowed he beckoned her forward, and said "Well! How do you like our collection? Does it meet with your approval?"

Julia was in heaven, all the paintings and sculptures she had so admired as an art student years ago seemed to be there (or at least copies). It was as if someone had seen into her mind and seen what she had chosen all those years ago.

"How could you know that I have loved and still love all these works?" She asked this in a hushed almost choked whisper, she was close to tears- it was as if someone had seen into her very soul.

"I chose these, because as a boy I lived in Firenze and saw all these beautiful works of art and I too loved them. I so much wanted to paint, to be an artist, to work at what I loved... but my father, he was a restaurateur and all he wanted was a load of waiters, which my mother gave him year after year after year.

My father was a very domineering man, and we all obeyed him whether we liked it or not. He ruled Julia, his wishes were always followed. So I became head waiter, and as a dutiful son I married the daughter of my father's wine merchant - she does not love me and she never has. She hates art, can't stand opera, she can't stand love making, touching or kissing, in fact she'd rather read a romance book or watch a film or gossip or anything, rather than have sex with me! So that's why I'm here- in my very own little Italy with all the things that I love."

Julia looked at him with sympathy, she'd always wanted to be an artist; had even got as far as Art college. Her father too was a strict, harsh controlling man, he'd gone to the college and told them he didn't like their modern art and could they not teach his daughter that sort of crap! So Julia went to teacher training college instead, and the nearest she got to fine art was fabric printing. Now she was a part time craft teacher at an Adult Education Centre, and had a fifty eight year old husband who'd forgotten all about sex, love and tenderness, preferring a game of golf and a pint with his golfing buddies. The rest of the time he spent in his office or asleep in front of the television or watching more golf. She had every sympathy with Antonio, and felt completely at ease with him.

He took her hand again and with his thumb gently wiped away a stray tear that had crept down her cheek; he leaned forward and kissed away the tear that was following. He smiled at her and led her through another set of very large black and gold doors as he said "I want to show you my copies of the De Vinci cartoons, in my private apartment and we must be alone."

Vittorio held Tanya close to him, he guided her past the paintings and statues to a very large recess with a long heavy and rich tapestry draped across it. He released her waist and with his strong arms and hands pulled the heavy tapestry back, and led her through into the dimly lit recess. He turned the subtle lighting a little higher and waving his hand he indicated his own magnificent workmanship.

A huge pure white glistening marble table with beautiful carved pillars stood in the centre, more an altar bed than a table, Vittorio ran his hands over the smooth marble, "Feel it mia Cara, and feel how it's as if it has life in it." He turned to her and said "You know it is said Michelangelo chose marble that had life in it for his sculptures!" Tanya was about to run her hand over the rim of the table, when Vittorio, just lifted her up high and laid her onto the table top pressing his lusty body against her. She could feel the cool smooth marble on her neck and arms.. And then her back, as Vittorio slid her dress off; it slipped down the surface of the table and then down one of the marble pillars and lay a crumpled heap on the floor. "Vittorio! No! No stop we mustn't I can't Oh! Stop Vittorio please oh!-oh!" Tanya's protests were slowly stopped by Vittorio kissing her and caressing her. He was almost moulding her neck and shoulders into the table. Her body sliding smoothly on the creamy white marble. He was kissing her down the nape of her neck and then very slowly he was slipping his tongue down to her breasts. He cupped his great hands round them and then placed his lips round a nipple and sucked very gently at first, till Tanya could feel herself sighing and gasping…Oh it was so sensuous.

Her whole body was tingling, moist, yet on fire, she could feel Vittorio lying heavy and hard at her side, his hands sliding down her back caressing the cheeks of her buttocks. He whispered "Let me explore you Tanya as I explore my marble, feeling for the life in you, searching every nook of you, till I feel you responding…ah! now I know you want me, I can feel the fluids of your soul flowing onto my hand, Oh mia Cara I must join you, let me pour my life juices into you, let me, let me."All Tanya could do was moan and sigh; she gasped an ecstatic "Oh! Yes! Yes! Yes Oh! God yes! "As she slid slowly up and down the marble table; and Vittorio mounted her entering her, flooding her with a deluge of his life juices till she could hold no more. Her whole body throbbed and pulsed, she was gasping and sighing as her thighs squeezed and shuddered together. Her back arched in an orgasmic spasm of pleasure.

Vittorio held her tight in his arms, he'd never seen a woman have such an orgasm before (and he'd had many women). "Tanya my Tanya you're wonderful" he whispered over and over as he tenderly kissed her.

Tanya began to relax and breath more easily, she stopped quivering with orgasmic delight and gradually became in control of her body. She looked at Vittorio and shook her head "I said no! I said no!"

"Yes but your eyes and your whole body said yes, and once I began the life in my marble took over" and Vittorio started to laugh as he lifted her off the table. She slipped away completely exhausted and utterly confused.

When she returned, Julia, Antonio and Vittorio were waiting, sitting on a large dark mahogany leather settee. There were four cups of cappuccino steaming on the nearby coffee table. Julia seemed quite excited (but not shocked at Tanya) as she said "Oh! Tanya Antonio and I have a great idea and I'm sure you and Vittorio will agree with it Antonio will outline it to Vittorio and I'll tell you on the way home in a taxi, we've indulged far too much to drive home.

They sipped their coffees while waiting for the taxi. Tanya wanted to talk but she was just too exhausted. She sat quietly while Vittorio held her hand, raising it and kissing it every few minutes. Julia spoke quietly with Antonio for some time, they seemed to be deep in thought and conversation as the taxi arrived. Antonio saw them to the taxi, and Julia turned as she got in saying "We'll see you tomorrow and I'll tell you yes or no, as we collect the car. "She sat back in the taxi and said" Number Eight Shady Lane," and then turning to Tanya "We'll stay at your place tonight and I'll tell you our plan."

Chapter Five.

The Ladies Who Do or The Italian Art and Culture Appreciation Society.

Julia looked at Tanya as she unlocked the front door and said "I knew those two wouldn't be awake so I've left a text on James mobile, and when they do wake they'll know where we are." Tanya just dropped into an easy chair, she felt too guilty to speak. Julia just shrugged her shoulders and said "Oh! Come on Tanya, I don't know what went on behind that tapestry, and I don't want to, that was your business and your revenge, just as what I did with Antonio is mine! O.K. Tanya. But we started to plan well an idea and it gives us the chance to break out from boredom and endless boring and wasted weekends waiting for golfers' to return!"

Tanya brightened visibly; this wasn't just going to be one wild evening of revenge after all. "Tell me I'm listening" said Tanya. Julia outlined the idea of a ladies culture group that would meet at Penguinos every fourth week to enjoy Italian food and arrange meetings to admire, discuss and taste Italian art, food ,wine and culture; these lively convivial events would be held at Penguinos in their beautiful art gallery; "Antonio will give a slide show and talk about some of Florence's well known sculptures for our first evening followed by a wine tasting and light supper." Julia pulled a questioning face at Tanya "Well what do you think? I've even planned a poster for the golf club, so James and Mark can pin it up and they'll know where and what we're doing while they're busy with golf!"

Tanya laughed "Gosh you were busy last night- did you spend all evening thinking this up? Or just a little time admiring the David's' body, his beautiful biceps and things!!-- I was admiring and stroking Italian marble, very sensuous, very smooth, and very! very! cool. But now, I'm exhausted so I'm off to bed to dream about marble, see you in the morning."

Tanya was walking towards the stairs, when Julia stopped her and asked "But do you think it's a good idea? And shall we tell them we'll go ahead tomorrow?"

"Oh! In for a penny in for a pound! Yes! At least it's a start" said Tanya.

They left the room quietly, and climbed the stairs to dream of Italy, paintings and statues and cool, cool marble. Meanwhile James and Mark slept obliviously on, dreaming of golf, and birdies and holes in one.

Chapter Six.

The Ladies Revenge Club, or Rather the Ladies Who Do Club.

Tanya took Julia to collect the car early next morning; she'd received a text from Mark it read "O.K. J & I going for 2nd round see you later kid".

"Oh! Mark! That was wrong…you should have asked what you are doing? You should have been cross or interested, or at least aware, not, definitely not, just ready to go off for another game of bloody golf." She thought.

Any tinge of guilt Tanya felt evaporated as she deleted the text message, now she was ready to help with the planning, and even ready for trips to Italy maybe even a visit or two to a marble quarry if possible.

When she pulled up beside Julia's car, Antonio and Vittorio were outside waiting, smiling and rushing forward to usher them into the restaurant. "Come on girls! Hot coffee and some warm Panini with eggs are ready and waiting." Antonio sat down at the table they had sat at the night before and the others joined him.

They ate and talked at the same time, it was so easy to plan and arrange, everything falling nicely into place. Julia had designed a poster with Antonio's help; it would be off the printer later in the morning. She could even take them up to Whittley Green Golf Club and place them on the notice boards if she got permission. The poster requested any lady wishing to join the group should please telephone Julia's mobile number or Tanya's for more details.

Tanya looked at Julia over her hot coffee and asked "What if no one rings do we still go ahead?" Julia pursed her lips and thought for all of ten seconds and said "Well if so it will be the society of two ladies who do that's all, but I'm sure I can recruit more bored golf widows especially with my poster and friendly persuasion." With that Tanya and Vittorio finished their coffee and eggs deciding to take a walk in the countryside just near to Whittley Green and then over the fells. Tanya turned to Julia as they left cheekily saying "We're going to discuss marble and its finer points --- ring me later, let me know how you get on at the golf club."

Julia and Antonio were left alone in the restaurant. She smiled at Antonio and said, "This is some sweet revenge! I hope Tanya doesn't get hurt or me for that matter!" "Well this is no innocent little flirtation is it?" enquired Antonio, Julia pondered on the question and turned it back on the questioner. "Well is it? And if not what is it to you?"

"You are not just a bit of fun, not a how you say? A one night stand, No, I have found a soul mate; you love the same things as me, and you crave affection and passion as I do. We will harm no one, we don't alter our family life, and we only grasp the moments to enjoy Italian art and culture. We are even willing to share it, so take the posters to the golf club and your husband and let's see what happens!"

An hour later Julia was parked outside Whittley Green golf club and thinking what she could say to James, when he emerged from the club house with Giles Smythe Dawson. They were both smiling and laughing, discussing their round of golf. James saw Julia and he waved to her, beckoning her over. "Well Hi! What do you know! The little misses has come to the golf club to find me, Have you missed me honey?" Julia gave her best forced smile while she inwardly seethed at the term "little misses" if any words were needed to iron her resolve to seek solace and revenge – they were it!

"I've come in search of the lady captain. I want permission to pin a poster in the ladies changing room and may be on the club notice board." Giles Smythe-Dawson leered forward, and came closer to her, he smiled lasciviously "Well clever girl, you've found the vice-captain instead, so let's see this poster and here what you're after. I'm sure I can help you little ladies."

Julia almost cringed, God they were so mind bogglingly condescending, so stupidly arrogant, chauvinistic, middle aged, gone to seed men. Julia fluttered her eye lashes and smiled a sweet girlie smile and in a breathy bimbo voice said "Oh! How utterly fantastic! I'm sure you'll persuade the lady captain and the club house steward too… you see my friend Tanya and I want to start a little club, an Italian art and culture and cooking club… to keep us amused and entertained whilst our husbands are on the golf course." She looked up at them and sighed sweetly all innocence and virtue, Giles Smythe-Dawson and darling James took the bait and laughed indulgently as they read the posters. They turned their backs on Julia and fairly ran into the club house.

Well if this club thingy kept the "little ladies" happy and "out of their hair ", they were all for it. More time for golf and even a round of drinks with the lads after. James, Giles, Jason Doupé and Mark could make up a really good foursome and maybe win the Captains Day tournament even…life was great, things in the golf club were really looking up and the "little ladies" wouldn't feel neglected or left out, in fact they should be encouraged whole heartedly to start this new little hobby as soon as possible. Giles would persuade his own little "Wifey" to join and Jason Doupé, well he'd think this club society thing was a godsend anything to get the wife out the way!

And so the bitter sweet revenge of the golf widows continued. They would relish the romance of Italy and the escapism it so seductively offered. Antonio Ullivari, art critic and restaurateur, would personally guide and encourage the organizer of this little enterprise and his larger than life pal Vittorio Tartaglioni marble master mason supreme would ensure that Julia's bosom companion Tanya would truly relish and appreciate the finer points of Italy's magnificent marble.

Julia and Tanya would be accompanied by a further four ladies, who would need their senses awakened to all the delights that the Ladies Italian Appreciation Society had to offer and perhaps a little more besides.

These ladies were encouraged to contact Julia by none other than Giles Smythe- Dawson, the golf club vice-captain. Giles was a merchant banker, although his staff and many of the golf club members knew him more as something that rhymed with it; but he was harmless really, in a male chauvinistic sort of way. He didn't realise just how helpful he was being to the Ladies who do Society. Ah well! He was a very proud and arrogant little man, but his pride was through the Ladies who Do Society, about to fall, even to plummet, and the revenge of his darling "wifey" would be discussed at great length round the marble table at Penguinos. Ella Dawson or "My own little Nigella" as Giles liked to call her was about to explain her revenge as a golf widow in the guise of "If you can't beat them join them and then beat them soundly!" All this sweet revenge was going to be recounted round a light pasta meal, and it was to be a revealing and amusing yet emancipating story that was to show Ella as a woman of outstanding qualities (and not all of them, the dutiful wifely qualities that Giles so fondly adored.)

Chapter Seven.

The Italian Society Discuss Buonarroti's David and Donnatellos David.

The following week Julia and Tanya introduced the four golf widows to Penguinos and the magnificent art gallery, and all the paintings, sculptures and of course the beautiful art décor marble furniture.

Antonio Ullivari was at his most charming Italian attentiveness, and delighted the ladies with his statuesque looks and his sensuously smooth yet husky voice. He was positively wooing the ladies as he showed image after image of Michelangelo's David, each image discussed with a growing sense of admiration and adulation. The ladies were entranced and completely won over. It was then that Vittorio Tartaglioni intervened saying "Oh ladies this is not the only David Florence is home to! Let me introduce you to my favourite David, Donatello's David. He's not nearly so big, but he is a beautiful essay of physical perfection sculptured in bronze, a young, sensual, fresh, nude boy; ah yes, you see, he stands so daintily on Goliaths head, his own little head so coquettishly tilted, a charming little hat accentuating his long curly locks that frame his pretty face . A charming smile on his cupid bow lips." At this point Vittorio and Antonio both laughed and Vittorio continued "Yes Donatello's David screams out to the viewer, there are other ways of killing a giant than with a sling!" Vittorio ventured, very sympathetically, that Donatello's David was perhaps one of the best statues of a homosexual nature there was. It had an indefinable erotic energy that didn't detract from its greatness but added to it, it was sensuous and flowing and very, very beautiful.

The ladies were laughing now, relaxed and warmed, they sipped a light dry *Friscati* and passed Amaretto biscuits around, all were enjoying these delightful nibbles, except,

Julia noticed Ella Smythe-Dawson. Yes she was laughing and engrossed with the descriptions of the statues, but she'd hardly touched any of the light meal or delicacies that lay on the table and she only sipped Pellegrino water, absolutely no alcohol passed her lips.

Julia and Tanya were intrigued by Ella Dawson, especially as they'd met Giles, and couldn't quite see how these two managed to be a married couple. Julia turned to Ella and smiling asked "well Ella I hope you've found this evening entertaining and informative and that you'll be part of our Ladies Italian Appreciation Society?"

Ella Dawson laughed a seductive laugh "Oh yes! I wouldn't have missed this evening, I've got to keep Giles happy, and whatever keeps Giles happy keeps me happy and that's what we ladies want don't we!?" "Oh yes, Tanya and I, have come to a conclusion; if we are happy then James and Mark can play as much golf as often as they want, in fact the more golf the better! You see Ella our interest is entirely taken up with things Italian, we're quite happy to share our absorbing interest with any lady that feels in need of extra curricula activities, and we are even willing to aid them in fulfilling their full potential in whatever sphere they desire to excel in."

"Oh right! Right I think I'd better fill you ladies in on my marital back ground and the journey we've travelled so far!" Thus it was that Ella Smythe-Dawson told her story over Amaretto biscuits and coffee, and the ladies listened in the soft warm lighting of the Italian Art and Culture Gallery, learning there are many ways to achieve success and overcome boredom, and it was Ella who was to enlighten them.

Chapter Eight

Ella Smythe-Dawson's Story.

It was once said that no control was firmer or more extensive than one that embraced the mind and will of its subject so successfully that opposition never reared its head, and so it was with Ella and Giles.

Indeed when Ella was first married she, for a time felt that she truly did have it all, a beautiful five bedroomed house, with double garage and rambling lawns. All maintained to perfection by Ella's fair hands and of course the occasional hired help that Giles voluntarily paid for whenever his dear Ella requested it. Add a handsome son, Jack and a stunningly beautiful daughter, Sophia, both intelligent and suitably accomplished thanks to an expensive private education, and one has the picture of perfection an ideal domestic vision of English family life.

Ella was indeed adored by Giles, as she was everything he desired in a woman. She was a natural beauty in the traditional English way, curvaceous in a Sophia Loren-esque manner. Her thick dark chocolate brown hair tumbled gracefully over her shoulders providing a subtle distraction to her large voluptuous breasts, a feature that Giles particularly enjoyed and adored. Her face was equally sensual, with large oval eyes the colour of hazelnut, thick long lashes, the envy of other women who resorted to falsies! To get the same look. But perhaps her best feature was her lips plump and moist, framing pearl like straight teeth, she truly was gorgeous. Sound familiar? Well Giles certainly thought of her as his very own Nigella Lawson as beautiful and sexy as the real Nigella, and as equally talented in the kitchen. In fact could a man have it any better? He certainly didn't think so.

His ideal day was a successful day at the bank bringing home the bacon so to speak, followed by a round of golf including some jolly good banter with the guys at the nineteenth hole, before retiring home at around 8.30pm to his darling Nigella, who would of course have made him a hearty meal, possibly with pastry and buttered potatoes and of course some delightful gooey dessert to finish the meal before taking his darling Nigella to the bedroom for a quick wham bam thank you mam! And this scenario was played out on a seemingly never ending daily basis in the Smythe-Dawson household. A truly self-indulgent, self-centred life style that Giles enjoyed as a pig enjoys wallowing in muck, ah well; he was a truly happy banker.

For Ella this arrangement had somewhat evolved over the years, but she didn't mind, she had contentment in being a homemaker and a domestic Goddess. Why should Giles involve himself in things that she could handle? And so many a parent's evening Ella had attended alone, but Giles had listened attentively when she relayed their children's talents to him over a glass of wine at supper. Or choosing a new item of furniture, it only irritated Giles and in any event it pleased Ella that Giles simply handed her over the finances to choose herself what would look good in the house, she was never wrong and Giles always approved of her choices, if he bothered to notice. The same was true of holidays, as long as the resort had a reputable golf course view, Giles was happy for her to book the holiday alone whilst his ideal day went on undisturbed by regular family life. But it was in the kitchen where Ella lost herself, she could lose hours concocting the most delicious and comforting meals that she would lovingly serve up for Giles and the children, no expense spared, the finest of ingredients with no real thought as to their calorific or fat content, why compromise on taste? And yet; one day Ella suddenly and inexplicably felt that she could no longer pull it off. At 40 she didn't feel curvaceous anymore, in fact she felt downright dumpy and (she could hardly dare to think it) but she had to admit that her arse was indeed fat! She worried whether Giles would still love her as her bottom got wider, and when he slapped her bottom these days the wobble carried on for a much longer period than she felt content with.

Then of course she had the unenviable indignity of seeing her svelte like 15 year old daughter skip about in skinny jeans and crop tops with nothing remotely muffin like hanging over, compare that to Ella's overhanging love handles with size 16 panties on, the picture was grim. No it was no good, if she was to keep her man she had to address the issue direct, and for the first time in her life Ella contemplated exercise.

The gym however was quite simply not Ella's cup of tea. The aerobics instructor had a nasal piercing for one thing, and it was an expensive gym, Ella was surprised that such types were actually allowed to make a living there! Then she actually used the term "Belly" for Gods' sake! Well, it was simply too much for Ella to bear. Such phraseology Ella felt should remain safely in a Northern circuit comedy club. Ella then tried a personal trainer, who set her up a programme in the gym, however Ella found the experience rather dull and felt that really one had to lose a decent amount of weight before she could actually reveal herself in the gym during the day. There were so many ladies who looked good, that she felt intimidated by them, especially in the changing room, too many thongs and pretty bras competing against Sloggies. So she tried swimming, but it was such a faff, and with Ella's hair being so thick, it was too time consuming and it cut into Ella's' hectic schedule of getting Giles' dinner ready. After trying power walking, which Ella found to be both boring and too taxing on her knees, Ella stumbled upon an idea that she felt would serve the purpose of her losing weight and would in the long term enhance her relationship with Giles. The plan was to surprise Giles by taking a secret course at the Golf Club. Of course, Ella would have to make up a little white lie to persuade Giles to give her the requisite cash to pay the fees, so she told him she was taking up sewing and would need the money to take a short home furnishing course. Giles duly agreed, as he would, he always took pride in his little wifey learning new skills. Blissfully he put his hand into his pocket and gave Ella all she needed to set herself up. Little did he know that his wife was about to embark upon a truly life changing venture and what a dramatic impact it would have upon him.

At first, Ella was nervous. She had no idea that Todd Horner Mann, the professional golfer imported from the USA, would have been quite so young. He did however; appear to have a very impressive resume, having won a fair amount of competitions in his heyday, now he raked in a good living, correcting the flaws in the swings of many a seasoned amateur at the Whittley Green Golf Club. Of course, during the day his working life was generally in encouraging the retired couples who had taken up golf in the twilight of their lives, and so when Ella arrived for her first lesson, her relative youth, in comparison to his usual clientele, was warmly received, very warmly.

Todd greeted Ella with a typical American broad grin. "Well how ya' doin' Mrs Dawson? Welcome to the Club".

"Oh please call me Ella."

"Well only if you call me Todd", which he pronounced in an elongated American way, Tarrrrd, Ella couldn't help herself, but had to repeat it American style, but inside she had a giggle to herself, as he really was a little hot Toddy!! Perhaps this was going to be a hoot after all!!

Todd took Ella straight away onto the driving range and set to work straight away making an assessment of her skills and abilities etc. Ella felt rather proud of herself as Todd remarked upon how much natural skill she had. He had a kind manner, bless him thought Ella, she bet he said that to all the ladies, particularly the rich ones.

She enjoyed Todd's muscular body behind her, as he helped her grasp the club handle in the correct manner, ready to address the ball. She felt strangely aroused by his hot breath as he explained in her ear, how to swing the club back and round, always keeping your eye focused on the flag. And he followed through, he must have felt the weight of her right breast on his arm, for he left his arm across it for some considerable time (or so it seemed!) as he looked straight into her eyes. He gently hummed and looked down at her heaving breasts, "I think may be we've got a little bit of a problem here" and he lovingly touched the tip of her bosom, "but nothing that you and I can't overcome. Let's go back to my pro shop and we'll talk about it!"

Oh Giles, Giles, if only you had tried to encourage little Ella on the golf course, instead, here she was in the hands of a rather handsome 34 year old, who knew all about women and their quests for the body beautiful. And he, Todd Horner Mann junior, was going to be the transformer of that body and the enabler of the most promising beginner that Whittley Green Golf Club had ever seen.

He told Ella that she had great potential and that he would enjoy being her very personal trainer on the course, he would iron out her swing problems and make sure she got the right elevation when she struck. He noted quite candidly that her swing was impeded by her large but beautiful bosom; this he could correct by an 'excellent low carb diet' he had brought from America (where many of the ladies had a similar problem) and by a really good sports bra that kept the beauties still while you swung, would she like to try one on? ...Now!!

Ella did, she slipped off her fine Nike top, to reveal a lacy bra all underwired, and completely wrong for the golf course, as Todd informed her. He walked into the changing cubicle and was eyeing her breasts with admiration and yet a critical golfing eye! He had just the right bra for her size 38 it didn't matter about cup size. They've got to be controlled, confined, moulded, and suppressed even. He handed Ella the sports bra and unfastened her pretty lace one, she gasped as he did so. Really this was going a bit too far even for a horny American, and she was about to admonish him in her most English manner, when he said "Look honey! I've seen more tits on the beaches of Acapulco than you've had hot dinners! So chill out! Be proud of 'em they're great! We just want to get 'em under control and down sized a little!"

Ella couldn't help laughing, from that moment on she'd hit it off with Todd and they were to scheme together on how she was to lose weight and be better at golf than Giles Smythe- Dawson ever was or could be.

That was four months ago and two dress and bra sizes smaller. She was now a hard swinging chick, and some of the men on the golf course were beginning to get quite envious of Todd, because she was some hot arsed little lady when she addressed the ball, in fact a pure joy to watch as she wriggled her cheeks and curvaceous hips.

Her son Jack and some of his sixth form college mates had evidently noticed the subtle transformation that was taking place. They were turning up at Giles house rather more frequently than they used to. Suddenly, studying for their mocks became really important. Ella thought it was for her home made snacks at first, but she felt more and more stared at lately, and as she left the study she heard the sighs, guffaws and exclamations. In the end she asked her daughter what these lads were up to, and could she explain what Miffy was or meant because one of his best friends kept calling her that?

Sophia just about wet herself laughing, and she patted her mother's trim peach like bottom and said "Oh mummy! You know you really should be proud and take that as a wonderful compliment; they think you're really something else!"

"What that cute little furry bunny thing, wasn't it a children's story, a children's TV programme, or something like that?" Ella genuinely didn't know, so Sophia sat her down and calmly but quietly informed her that Miffy was not the cute little rabbit on TV, no it was a nomenclature, a list similar to M.I.L.F. i.e. M.I.F.F.Y" "And what's that?" asked Ella . Sophia grinned, and whispered quickly as she began backing out of the room "Well M.I.L.F. stands for… Mother I'd like to fuck and M.I.F.F.Y. stands for Mother I fancy fucking you!" Ella was mortified, these boys were actually saying this about her, 17 and 18 year olds fancying her Oh no! Well hang on, well, maybe, yes it was a compliment and Ella began to laugh, her body had certainly improved!

Giles too was beginning to notice the changes at home, his evening meals that he truly loved, his Nigella specials, succulent, enticing; mouth-watering feasts well where were they lately? He longed for Ella's sumptuous 'beef in ale - flaky pastry pie' with her mouth-wateringly delicious homemade chunky chips, followed by her absolutely scrumptious homemade lemon meringue pie, Oh where were they?

It wasn't that Ella didn't provide evening meals, beautifully cooked ones at that, but of late they didn't seem to fill him, No pies, no chips, no pastry, no calorific content what so ever! He'd even taken to buying the odd meat pie and chips at the golf club to satisfy his craving for pies, and now he was sneaking large quantities of chocolate bars in the car and in the drawers of the bedroom. He was not the happy chappy he had been a few months ago.

Sex wasn't the same either; Ella seemed to want more, holding him to her and wriggling about, sighing and begging for more, well she never used to do that, she was always quiet and passive and still, as she should be! He was now quite exhausted when he'd had sex with her, in fact to be truthful he wasn't enjoying it at all. He was spending more and more evenings at the golf club to compensate for the loss of pies and chips and to escape the exhaustion of the bedroom! It was a jolly good job that Julia and Tanya had come along with this art and culture thing; maybe Ella would start to make pies again or something and start being still in the bedroom!

Ella looked up from her black coffee and said "So you see I've discovered a new slimmer, sexier, me, and one that enjoys playing golf; incidentally Todd thinks I'll be good enough to enter the captains day tournament, he even thinks I've a good chance of winning, so I'm having to go for lots of extra golf tuition and things! On and off the golf course! So you see ladies I need the Italian society to invite me out as often as possible, will you help me appreciate the finer things in life and fulfil my full potential?"

Julia and Tanya were smiling in admiration and appreciation. Ella was truly gorgeous, a beautiful figure and sparkling conversationalist, and an apparently gifted and talented golfer, who was going to reveal her new talent at the captains day dinner in July. The Ladies who 'do' couldn't wait.

In the meantime more Italian evenings needed to be planned.

"Perhaps we could maybe try some Italian cookery, I'd like to know how to make real pasta." Tracey Doupé suggested, very timidly, Ella, Julia and Tanya gave encouraging nods and smiles. Yes this little shrinking violet needed all the help and encouragement she could get and they the ladies who do were going to give that to her, it became Ella Smythe-Dawsons *reason d'etre.*

Tracey Doupé was the wife of Jason Doupé who was strutting and parading round the golf greens thinking he was God's gift to women and Whittley Green Golf course. Ella didn't think so, and by the looks of this cowed, brow beaten lady, neither did she. Tracey needed encouragement and pleasure and joy and fulfilment, she wasn't getting any of these things from Jason Doupé. The Ladies Italian Art, Culture and Cookery Appreciation Society were about to emancipate yet another golf widow and bring some sunshine into the life of a forgotten shy faded English rose. Cookery was going to awaken this lady's emotions and give her true pleasure, something she had never really tasted with Jason. She was going to blossom and bloom in the warmth of the Italian society, bathed in the light of encouragement of the wonderful Italian chef.

Chapter Nine

Tracey Evolves from a Shrinking Violet.

Julia, Tanya and Ella felt sorry for Tracey, she looked so dull, grey and insipid, there seemed to be no fire in her, as if years of neglect had caused her to fade into the background. She was small, slim and pale. Her hair was mousey and her face although a pretty oval shape lacked lustre and vibrancy. Her eyes were always down cast and she rarely looked anyone full in the face, a pity that, as her eyes were vibrant-violet blue.

Ella wanted Tracey to open up to 'chill out' as Todd would say, so she encouraged Tracey to suggest some more ideas about Italian Cuisine. Food and the making of it had once been Ella's passion, and she was able to describe some of her favourite pasta dishes with an almost sensuous pleasure. Tracey listened with an angelic Mona Lisa smile and a very pretty rosy blush on her cheeks.

Julia and Antonio watched and both noticed how this lady was very slowly lowering her guard and opening up to the pleasure of shared company. Antonio leaned over to her and suggested that their next meeting should be of a culinary nature. He would ask his very talented pasta chef to demonstrate making pasta. The chef would be available next Friday said Antonio "so yes ,Tracey you can make pasta, it's fun making pasta, you must mix it and knead it with love and pleasure. "Antonio smiled at Tracey "say yes that you will be apprentice pasta maker and we will all applaud you…yes?" Oh gosh poor Tracey the centre of attention, gentle caring attention, non-critical and encouraging. She blushed with pleasure and felt a tinge of excitement. "Well if you think it's alright and that I won't be to slow and clumsy… I'd love to have a try; yes I'd like that, if it's alright with you all?" And for the first time Tracey looked up and around the group, her eyes shining almost pleading for acceptance, as she made eye contact. Vittorio gasped at their iridescent beauty… "Darling you will give us all immense pleasure! Especially me! For I love to watch woman kneading and squeezing dough it is so very feminine, tactile and sensuous… I'm getting excited just thinking about it!" Tanya laughed as she saw Tracey now glowing with a very rosy blush and to save her further embarrassment she said "Oh Tracey take no notice, this man is just obsessed with anything female and tactile... as I know to my cost!"

Tracey was beginning to shrink back to close in on herself becoming her usual timid confused self. Ella stepped in, this must not happen, so she said "Tracey you and I are going to meet at the golf club…I've seen you there you've got quite a powerful swing and grip on your clubs, I think you'll knead that dough with an iron hand in a velvet glove. So we'll meet on Sunday at the club…but remember Tracey, Giles mustn't know!" Tracey gave Ella a grateful smile, "Oh I'd love that, but Jason doesn't like me going with him to the club... he says I cramp his style and get in the way."

Ella guffawed and snorted, but she smiled sweetly and said "Look honey (she was sounding more like Todd every day) I said Giles mustn't know…and neither must Jason… don't tell…I'll collect you in my car and we'll leave that in Todd's garage…we'll practice our swings, grips and elevation and then discuss culinary delights over *insalata di radicchio e rughetta* Jamie Oliver style O.K."

Tracey beamed saying "Oh I'd love to" and so it was settled, and the evening closed.

Julia and Tanya stayed after the others left. They admonished Vittorio for scaring their new found friend, "Look she's been brave enough to come here on her own and she's even going to stand up in front of us and maybe make a mistake or two, so I hope your chef is going to be ultra-gentle, and above all else ultra-sympathetic to Tracey!" Julia looked at Vittorio and Antonio inquiringly. Antonio placed his hand on Julia's shoulder saying "Leave this with me... I'll ensure that my chef treats Tracey with tender loving care. One problem though; the chef is Italian and speaks very little English, but I'll be a very gentle translator O.K." With that Vittorio and Antonio and the girls sipped a cappuccino with brandy and admired again the D.V.D's of Florence's David's. This Italian society was a very compassionate and indulgent affair and in every sense pleasurable.

Ella meanwhile took Tracey, Norma Gibson and Karen McNaulty on a long drive home. Norma and Karen were dropped off quite early, Ella thought they were incredibly boring, almost the undead because they had never lived, or so it seemed to her; but more about these ladies later, much later. Now her task was Tracey, she was going to find out why she was so timid and so lacking in confidence. All she had to do was listen and encourage…Tracey was about to tell all.

"You know I was only eighteen when I met Jason at college, I was a good little catholic virgin studying for my A levels, French, Italian and English literature. My dad was really proud of me, he'd brought me up single handed as my mum had died before I was two. He wanted me to have everything… but he didn't know how to show affection I suppose, and I so much wanted to be loved and admired."

Ella drove very slowly, she didn't want to interrupt but felt she needed to ask some questions "And did Jason give you that?" she asked.

"Oh, Jason was every female students dream, Ella, he was so macho and handsome in a James Dean sort of way, all smouldering and so mature, he wasn't just a student, he was an apprentice on day release for car mechanics, he was so grown up and all the girls desired him. So when he made a pass at me! I was thrilled, and all the girls envied me. He'd been asking about me they said, and wanted to get to know me. So I was putty in his hands as he sweet talked me into his shiny jag. He seduced me on our first date… in the back seat of his second hand Jag, he was so rough, forcing me he wouldn't stop, I struggled for a while, but he kept on going, forcing me back on the seat …he tore off my knickers and well you know what he did…I cried so much afterwards I think he was scared I'd tell; so he said he'd go out with me."

Ella was listening and watching Tracey, she was wringing a hanky tightly in her hands, "What happened then?" Ella quietly asked.

Tracey sighed deeply, "He met my dad and they seemed to get along like a house on fire. Jason could charm the hind leg off a donkey, and he sweet-talked like the clever, car salesman he is .Before I knew it dad had offered him a job in his garage showroom… It all seemed well, till I started being sick, yes, you've guessed it, a little Doupé was on the way. Well, Jason was well and truly trapped, my dad was heartbroken, his little angel was pregnant and she was going to do so well! Ah well! Jason was confronted and bribed with ownership of the salesroom and surprise, surprise a marriage took place, a good catholic marriage and a son was born. Jason has never forgiven me; we are an old married couple at thirty six. He's still handsome and the business keeps him in the style he wants…a fast Mercedes convertible, a fat wallet and a big bank account, Italian designer clothes and a Botox smooth face. The only thing he hasn't got is an attractive sexy looking wife who's good in bed."

Ella huffed and pushed back her hair "And he thinks he'll find that on Whittley Green Golf course! Tracey you are as attractive as you feel… and I reckon you haven't felt that for eighteen years! Honey you are coming with me for a makeover and then golf lessons? And don't let that swine of a husband stop you!"

"But can't you see! I don't want to have sex with him! I said he was rough when he seduced me, well he still is…he only enjoys my body when he's… knocking me around, he can't be normal, he's cruel and for some reason he has to be dominant, aggressive, brutal even; so I've tried not to be what he wants, I've tried to be in the background and if I could I'd melt away." Tracey was sitting very still her face expressionless, except for a few tears rolling slowly down her cheeks.

Ella was seething, she breathed heavily and then through clenched teeth she said "The bastard, he's a sadistic bully! You know what; Tracey that man must have a small prick… That's his problem not yours… Why don't you leave him, divorce him, don't try and please the little dick head!"

"I can't do that… don't you see my dad's a good old Irish catholic , he said at the start of our marriage, you made your bed, now for good or ill you must lie in it. So I try not to be noticed, while Jason spends more time preening himself and trying to be Mr big at the golf club. Our son is becoming more like him, a right little bully, and I'm so lonely, fed up and unloved I guess I'm desperate enough to take to drink, or worse!"

Ella stopped the car took Tracey firmly by the shoulders and said "God Tracey don't do that, you've got friends now, we'll help you, don't let that bastard grind you down! Now do you think you can last out till Sunday….. Look

I'll ring you tomorrow and we'll make arrangements. Just make sure Jason leaves for the golf club before we do!"

On Saturday Ella phoned Julia and Tanya and told them about Tracey's sad marital life. Well they all thought their husbands were boring golf crazy old men, but at least they weren't violent; and for all their mindless uncaring behaviour, there was no malice or intent to harm. Jason Doupé was sadistic, manipulative, and a money grabbing evil swine and he meant to hurt. Tracey would have their support, and be guarded, but some form of assistance had to be organised for her. They'd have to discuss the matter over pasta, a lot of pasta.

On Sunday Todd was wonderful with Tracey. Ella had quickly told him of Tracey's unhappy matrimonial predicament, his comment at the end was revealing "Jason Doupé, that little prick, he drives a Merc convertible, it's his penis extension; just like his golf clubs, Honey! He swings um around but he can't get the shot in the hole! If you know what I mean; he thinks he's one of the big guys like Giles. They just can't hack it Honey, just can't hack it…Now let's get you ladies on the golf course and swinging your arses and stroking those balls!"

Tracey was, by the end of the session, feeling happier. She was much more confident when she left Ella's house. Ella had persuaded Giles to have Sunday lunch at the golf club with his golfing partners Jason, Mark and James. Ella started the process of building Tracey's confidence. First a facial, massage and make up in the gym beauty shop (thank God it opened on Sunday) surprising what a difference make up can do for a girl; Tracey looked and felt like a makeover queen.

Later they sat in Ella's conservatory eating anti pasta and rocket salad as they discussed how to avoid Jason and Giles on the golf course and more importantly how to enter the ladies doubles tournament in July. Yes things were beginning to change for Tracey… she was beginning to fight back.

Meanwhile Giles and Jason *et al* were having a rough time, business wise and golf wise. This credit crunch and recession was causing major upheavals and severe financial worries. All four men were stressed and irritated at work, Giles particularly, his bank was in deep doodoo and rationalization programmes were going to take place… He couldn't concentrate and as a result his golf was even more inadequate than usual. He and Jason had almost come to blows at the 16th, Jason accusing him of moving the ball out of the rough. Giles would never do that! He might do a bit of creative accounting at the bank, but he was a true gentleman on the green and he would never cheat.

It was no surprise then that Jason returned home in a foul mood, and Tracey trying to be sympathetic offered him a treat of chocolate pudding and chocolate custard, and got the full force of his vile temper. The dessert flew through the air missed her, just, and hit the wall. Her left ear, neck and shoulder didn't however miss his Armani belt that flew through the air a number of times; fortunately the large ornate buckle hit the wall and ripped into the expensive wallpaper and not into her skin. Tracey made a fast exit and locked herself in the bedroom, while Jason screamed obscenities at her. He'd well and truly lost it this time.

Tracey could hear Jason's taunts and abuse start to change as the evening wore on, but she did not risk leaving the sanctuary of her bedroom. Her ear, neck and shoulder were swelling and aching. Tracey knew that this situation could not continue she must speak to her father and beg him to let her return home.

A lot later she crept out of the house and drove to the nearest A and E hospital. The triage sister was so very gentle with her, and asked how the wheals had been caused. Tracey couldn't speak, tears poured down her face. The sister obviously experienced in these "domestics" as she called them, told her the department would photograph the bruising and swellings, she firmly advised her to seek police help.

She returned home sad and weary and still in considerable pain, only to find a tearful and contrite Jason waiting at the door. He wouldn't do that ever again! "Ever, honest." He was just so stressed with the financial state of the business. He was staring at her, pacing round and round her. Tracey shook her head and wearily said "I'm going to bed Jason… just leave me alone, leave me alone!"

Tracey kept herself well out of Jason's way, deliberately avoiding him. She went to work wearing a high polo-necked jumper and for once she wore a lot of make-up. Her work colleagues said how much the make-up suited her and the jumper and scarf framed her face well. Tracey smiled they didn't have a clue as to how much was concealed beneath both. She tried phoning her father but didn't get any answers, until on Thursday he rang her and to Tracey's consternation asked "What's happened between you and Jason, Tracey, he says you won't speak to him or see him… 'cos you've had a little bust up… He's sorry Trace and he wants me to ask you to forgive him, he loves you Tracey, go on can't you forgive him." Tracey's heart sank, she sighed deeply and said in a quiet weary voice "I can't forgive him and I know exactly how he feels about me." She put the phone down and went wearily to bed. She was so looking forward to the salvation of the Italian society and the indulgence of pasta making.

Ella collected Tracey at 7.30; she noted the heavy makeup and the new hair style framing her face in a long bob. The beautiful silk cravat also highlighted her violet blue eyes. "Tracey you look great!" Ella said and she meant it. She didn't know that all this new appearance was to conceal the scars and bruises, both physical and mental, that Jason had lately inflicted on her. By the time they reached Penguinos Tracey had told Ella everything and that she was looking for a bolt hole. She didn't go into details about the argument or about her father's phone call and his request that she forgive Jason.

Ella knew that all was far from well, but she also saw that Tracey was beginning to assert herself and find her own solutions to her problems. The Italian society was waiting, they would support and encourage her, but Tracey would stand on her own two feet.

Antonio Ullivari invited the ladies to gather round the large marble table. He gave a light hearted and entertaining talk about pasta and the hundreds of different ways it can be served. He described his own childhood memories of watching his grandmother making pasta and how to this day he enjoyed a simple dish of plain spaghetti and meatballs.

Vittorio then went to the kitchen and returned with their talented chef, "Ladies please welcome Penguino's very own Master pasta chef Toni Borghini." He held out his large mason hand and drew forward a tall, young chef in checked harlequin trousers and a crisp white jacket and a checked bandana to match. The chef's face was incredibly scarred and red. The chef bowed to everyone and smiled as Tracey was ushered forward. Antonio introduced her to Toni in Italian saying how she Tracey was shy and to be gentle with her, when to everyone's surprise Tracey said in fluent Italian "I'm really looking forward to making pasta with you and please forgive me if I make mistakes. "The chef's heavily scarred face lit up and in a husky Italian voice Toni said *"Oh! Moltobene, bene."*

There followed, to everyone's enjoyment and amusement, an instant master chef class in Italian and an instant English translation by Tracey.

Toni took some very finely sieved flour and half a dozen free range eggs and placed them on the marble table. Toni explained to Tracey you make a mountain of the flour no a volcano, and then crack all the eggs into it, mix the flour into it till it's firm but not sticky. Tracey repeated the procedure; soon there were two large portions of dough on the table. Toni stood behind Tracey and leaned round her shoulders, "Now you must flour your hands and begin to knead, you can let yourself go, pull, squeeze and knead, like this,"

Toni's arms slipped through Tracey's and started gently to pummel the elastic dough, Toni whispered in Tracey's ear "You have fine strong arms and hands don't be afraid, be rhythmic and flowing." Tracey winced Toni had touched her ear and shoulder, she pulled back a little, Toni looked at her and moved her hair slightly and 'tutted', (no more was said) but the chef stroked Tracey's arms very gently and smiled encouragement, whispering all the time in Tracey's ear "you are so brave *cara* let me help you!" Tracey didn't translate this to the others ,she just felt her face tingling and a rosy hue came slowly rising over her cheek., Toni asked in a hoarse trembling voice warming Tracey's neck and ear with hot garlicky breath " Let me see what has happened to you!... come we go into the kitchen… we make mussels with pasta!" Tracey translated "We're going to make you some mussels in sauce to go with the pasta; this will take about half an hour!"

Toni said "Please have vino and anti-pasta while waiting O.K."

Tracey was whisked off with the pasta and rushed to the warmth of the restaurant kitchen.

The kitchen staff stepped back as Toni barked orders "plenty mussels in Sicilian sauce and some *carbonara* go make!" Toni pulled off the bandana to reveal long dark auburn flowing locks; Yes! the chef was an Italian woman with smouldering black eyes that were almost piercing into Tracey's violet blue ones. "Show me! Show me" she exclaimed, she took Tracey's hand and fairly dragged her through the kitchen to the dark store room. Toni pulled Tracey gently to her, raising her hair and removing the pretty cravat. Tracey closed her eyes and allowed the tears to fall, while Toni began gently kissing soft gentle kisses along the sore red wheel marks on Tracey's ear and neck. Tracey sighed and an overwhelming feeling of pleasure engulfed her. Toni whispered huskily "come home with me Tracey, come home. "And Tracey whispered "yes."

They returned to the group with a number of very delectable, immensely edible pasta dishes and everyone including Tracey ate with gusto, sucking the mussel juices up and dipping the pasta strands into various sauces. Julia noticed Toni wipe juice from Tracey's chin with her finger, she even put it in Tracey's mouth and Tracey licked it gently. "Mm! Well good for you Trace...Whatever turns you on and makes you happy go for it!" She said this quietly under her breath but Antonio heard and whispered back "Yes, I agree, but, please don't let her steal my chef; she really is the master in the kitchen! I suppose this had to happen, Toni has been looking for someone to love and to take care of for some time. She's always wanted to drink from the furry cup, this one is a little damaged, so much the better for Toni she'll lick her wounds dry and make her happy."

"Oh! You Italians you're totally besotted with love and passion…   I guess that's why I can't resist you! "Julia laughed indulgently.

It was no surprise to anyone to see Tracey leave with Toni. Ella raised her iced water and said to Toni "Look after her! She's going to be my doubles partner...on the golf course that is! I'll give you a lift Norma O.K."

With that the ladies left, all save Julia and Tanya, they needed to discuss the next Italian evening! *Cappuccino's* and *Torte di more* and brandy, a little gentle music, and a very pleasant evening came to a relaxing end, yes, the Italian, Art Culture and Cuisine Society was a super club to be in.

Chapter Ten.

A Brief Affair.

Toni took Tracey home in a clapped out old red mini, they arrived in recession declining Coppull. Toni's flat was above a fish and chip shop, down a narrow Victorian back street. But at this moment in time it was a very comforting safe haven. Toni had cleaned it and painted it white, she'd covered the battered old bits of furniture and single bed with bright woollen throws and garish cushions, the effect was quite pleasing, although at this moment Tracey didn't notice.

Toni held Tracey's hand and led her to the small bed, she slid Tracey's soft cashmere jumper off and gave a gasp of outrage, Tracey's shoulder was still very swollen and purple bruises covered her neck and shoulder. The belt had left deep indentations in her skin around her neck and ear. Toni put her hands gently round Tracey's waist and drew her close, she began to very softly kiss her ear and neck and Tracey began to relax, her eyes were closed and she was gently swaying to and fro. Toni laid her back on the bed and quietly, gently, like a tender mother she undressed her, she was crooning in Italian "I'm going to look after you baby, I'm going to make you better now, so hush don't you worry now ,Toni look after you now."

She warmed the soothing aromatic oil and started to gently massage Tracey's neck and shoulders in soft feathery circular movements. She continued the movements over the aching bruised welts. Tracey began to sigh with relief, "Oh! That's wonderful it's so nice, and it doesn't hurt!" she whispered. Toni continued massaging downwards, slowly down her spine and rib cage, and then even more slowly and gently she put her warmed oily hands on Tracey's heaving breasts. She smoothed the warm oil round Tracey's erect nipples, and with her fingers she massaged the rosy red erect nipples till Tracey began to moan in an ecstasy of pleasure, she had never ever, ever felt like this. She desperately wanted more. Toni kissed her wounded neck, began to lick the marks with her long pink velvety soft tongue, moving from her neck to her heaving breasts. She began to run her tongue round the rosy erect nipples and playfully sucked them. Tracey was writhing in pleasure, gasping in anticipation.

Toni sank her head between Tracey's parted legs and sank her tongue deep into her mound of Venus, her long tongue thrusting and searching for Tracey's G spot. Tracey arched her whole body, squeezing her thighs round Toni's head. She had never realized what an orgasm was until now, her whole body tingled and throbbed in a crescendo of sexual delight ,wave after wave, spasm after spasm engulfed her in sensual pleasure, she felt fulfilled at last.

They fell asleep in each other's arms in the little single bed, sleeping like innocent children, naked content and exhausted, all passion spent, they slept.

Tracey awoke to the buzzing of her mobile phone; she leaned over Toni and pressed the receiver … it was Jason. "Tracey where are you? Please Tracey speak to me! For God's sake women speak to me!" Tracey didn't answer and Toni put her arms round her reassuringly. "Tracey, Tracey speak to me! You're killing me! You bitch you bitch come back!" Jason's voice was getting more and more demanding he was shouting over and over again speak to me! And in a maniacal scream he yelled "Bitch, bitch you're killing me!" Toni picked up the mobile and switched it off.

Tracey turned to Toni, saying, "He has such a nice way with words, my husband; I really must speak to him… later; much later."

The girls ate warmed teacakes and drank steaming hot milky chocolate in bed, enjoying each other's company and speaking Italian. Toni hadn't understood Jason's words but the shouting and screaming had conveyed enough anger and threats, to make her scared for Tracey. She wanted to protect her, but it was Tracey who suggested that Toni return with her to the matrimonial home, "You can be my lodger, and Protector Toni!" Tracey was confused and consumed by the sense of guilt she felt that their love making had produced. Her strong catholic upbringing made her feel ashamed, yet she knew that this young woman felt more for her than Jason ever could or would. Their marriage was a sham…it provided Jason with a financial background, and the key to all the right places he wanted to be in. As for Tracey, well she was his meal ticket and occasional punch bag and kinky sex toy that he liked to punish.

So Tracey asked Toni to be her friend and companion, she would have her own rooms in the Doupé house; she would be there to watch over and protect Tracey. Toni felt for Tracey, she had suffered enough cruel brutalizing abuse in her own childhood, by a father who saw women as mere vessels for sadistic sexual gratification; She, Toni Borghini would never love a man, never have a man near her! So if she could not be Tracey's lover to be Tracey's protector and friend was enough.

Chapter Eleven.

In Vino Veritas.

Julia and Tanya sat with Antonio and Vittorio sipping their cappuccinos and trying to decide what would be a good theme for their next meeting. Vittorio wanted to look at beautiful women, especially naked beautiful women. Julia gave him a withering look and informed him "The ladies Italian Art and culture society had a rather more sophisticated and cultured view of the female form, but perhaps a look at Titian's Venus of Urbino might be appropriate." "Yes I can give you some art historian's explanations about his work, but I think we need something more for the evening." Said Antonio.

It was at that moment, Ella returned with Norma Gibson. "Would you believe it the car won't start …. I'd left the side lights on. Sorry." Ella looked really cheesed off and so did Norma, who turned to Antonio and asked "is it alright if I use your phone? …I'll have to wake Rodney and get him to collect us." Norma was not like the other ladies in the Italian society, no; she was not! She was a rather plump, suburban, greying elderly housewife with her typical Marks and Spencer's twinset and pearls. Her hair was permed and it was set in the back and bubbly style of the early seventies (could she really be as boring as she looked.)

Ella sat with Julia and Tanya and the men, they were continuing their discussion about the Titian painting and how the lady looks as though she is waiting for an amorous adventure. Vittorio said it was in the eyes and the provocative come hither pose that she holds, it was so sexual and sensual, he loved that painting.

Norma stood behind him, waiting, arms folded, she tutted and looked up to heaven. "Well, Rodney's going to get up and come for us, but it'll take some time as he's to get his joints going and the car as well for that matter!" Vittorio smiled in a bemused manner and asked Norma and Ella if they would like coffee. Ella said "I'd love one," but Norma surprised everyone saying "I won't drink coffee it'll keep me awake… all that caffeine, no, can I try some of that there Barolo we had earlier, I really, really liked that! "Antonio ever the gentleman, poured coffee for Ella, and a large goblet of Barolo Reservee for Norma. He explained to Norma the history of this exceptional and very expensive wine, she sipped it and smiled and was absolutely entranced by the story.

"Now you've really captured my interest!.. Yes I'd love to hear more about wine and that sort of thing. All that art and sex sort of thing, well it's alright ,I suppose in its way, if you like that sort of thing, but it leaves me cold,… all that sort of thing, well it all stops at forty, thank goodness!"

Julia, Tanya and Ella's mouths dropped very quietly open, was this lady for real, they really must find out more about her! Vittorio almost choked on his cappuccino and coughed to hide his suppressed laughter. Only Antonio remained externally calm and controlled, he tilted his head and said "Ah I'm so glad we have found what really interests you from Italy; - Is there anything else besides wine?"

Norma took another long draft of the Barolo sighed heavily and smiled leaning over towards Antonio, she whispered breathlessly "Well if you must know, I just love wine and cheese, and Serona ham and some of those anti – pasta things! Oh! Yes I get really excited with a good cheese… you know one that you can sink your teeth into and it leaves teeth marks! You know a Gorgonzola of a cheese…Mm oh yes I'd love that." Norma's eyes closed and a look of pure bliss passed over her face…yes that was Norma's heaven. "But Rodney won't entertain any cheese but English cheese…none of that foreign stuff, he says he won't have it in the shop…no, only English cheese…and pies and pasties. He's very set in his ways is Rodney…Very set in his ways."

It was at that moment that Rodney knocked on the locked door of Penguinos; and Vittorio ran to let the old gentleman in, and his huge belly laughter out.

Rodney was entirely suited to Norma, they complimented each other perfectly. He was about 5ft 6ins, and quite stooped in the back, he had a small oval pale face with a hint of greying stubble on his chin and cheeks, he wore gold rimmed glasses that lodged on a large beaked nose, he also wore a camel coloured flat cap from which a few wisps of grey curls escaped. He was expressionless. He wore grey flannel trousers, a pale blue shirt and a Fair Isle cardigan that buttoned down the front. He was very set in his ways and he looked it!

He and Norma were married in 1964, he wore grey flannel trousers then, and he was wearing them still, perhaps not the same pair, but the style and colour were exactly the same. "I know what I like, so why change. "This was Rodney's creed. He had lived all his life in Bestwood and he had grown used to its quiet back water ways. He had met Norma at the local Methodist church, she was a girl guide he was a scout. They were good, honest and upright (and a deviant naughty thought never entered their innocent heads.) They were both virgins when they married, 22 years old and innocent, and now over 40 years on they were still sexually naive and innocent. Rodney was not demanding and he didn't crave or lust after anything, in fact he just liked a quiet life; and Norma never having been aroused, and accepting her aged mothers philosophy of "lie back and think of England! And all that stops at forty!" Norma's sexual feelings had wilted and atrophied. So they had no children, no pets (because of Rodney's allergies) and absolutely no interests except for their cheese shop and their weekly game of golf…. But then some people are easily satisfied and pass through life only half awake.

Norma introduced Rodney to Antonio and the others, Rodney shook hands with Antonio with a rather soft, clammy palm. "Oh very nice place you've got here Mr Antonio... very nice, although Italian stuff isn't my cup of tea....still, very nice....right are you ready Norma, 'cause if we've to take Mrs Dawson back it'll be a long drive." "Oh gosh! Don't worry about me Rodney, I'll get a taxi later O.K.! "Ella smiled wide eyed and bushy tailed...she didn't want to spend too long with Rodney, boredom might kill her!

Norma smiled so sweetly and she hugged Ella, "Oh you're such a love! So kind and considerate, you're all lovely, lively, ladies and I must say I've really enjoyed this Italian society... and that Barolo! Well I Know you don't like wine Rodney... but that Barolo! Ohm it made my tongue tingle and my toes turn especially when Mr Antonio talked about it!" Norma started to gently chuckle.. She put her arm round Rodney's arm smiled sweetly at every one and said "come on Chuck! Time for you and me to hutch up in bed.... Bye!"

The gentle elderly couple waved from the car as it moved slowly off. Vittorio just sank into the large leather sofa and began to cry with laughter. "Don't!" said Tanya "They're in a different time zone than us, and I won't let you take the urine out of them!" Antonio smiled at Tanya as he poured out some more Barolo and sipped it. "You know you're quite right they are definitely in another age, very like my mother and my wife; but I think deep down there inside Norma, there lurks a longing to be aroused." Julia laughed "What do you think our Norma is then? A right little goer! As they say up North!" Antonio shook his head "No, no she's a lovely lady, she is all innocence, but I think she could, well, enjoy life a little more.. She loves her husband and she does what will please him, so we must encourage her to please him!"

"Yes but the only thing that awakens Rodney is Cheese!" Ella raised her shoulders and with that remark, went out tried her car again, it started first time. "I'll leave you to ponder on how we can get Norma to please Rodney and enjoy life a little more... I think that's definitely a big challenge,

55

you're more likely to awaken the Donatello David. I'll phone Tracey tomorrow to make golf arrangements… ring me later in the week. See you!" With that Ella left.

Antonio asked Julia to talk to Norma and to encourage her to bring some English cheeses to their next meeting. He would persuade Carlo Poncepé, his vintner and delicatessen supplier to bring a selection of fine wines, cheeses and antipasti; they could have a taste-in and a competition for the strongest tasting cheese. Julia thanked Antonio, it was a good idea, all she'd got to do was to win Norma and Rodney over, and that was a challenge.

Julia rang and rang Norma's home line, but there was no answer, and rather than wait she decided to visit the cheese shop, where the two Lancashire cheese lovers were. Surprise, surprise it was called the Lancashire Cheese Shop. It was a small neat, plain, no frills cheese shop, it was however very clean and not expensive.

The cheeses were stacked in neat rows, ranging from a very white Lancashire crumbly to a very orange Black sticks blue veined.

There were no foreign cheeses at all. The only other foods on offer were Butter pies, meat and potato pies, Lancashire hot pot, mince and onion peppered pasties. You could almost hear Rodney saying I know what I like, so we'll sell what I like.

Norma stood behind the counter near the till, a little white cap and hairnet over her grey hair, a salmon pink overall covered her powder blue twinset. Rodney stood nearby in a white flat cap and a white overall over his cardigan and grey flannels, his hands were behind his back Duke of Edinburgh style. He turned his head towards her as she entered the shop but there was no sign of recognition from Rodney. Norma however squeaked with delight "Oh Julia do come on over, what can we do for you?"

"Norma, Rodney it's what we the Ladies Italian Society, can do for you!" and with that she waved a large bottle of Barolo Reservee… "Have you by any chance some really delicious strong tangy tasty cheese and of course some glasses!" Norma grinned broadly and ran into the back of the shop and returned with three tumblers. "Oh! God! No! I can't give you Barolo in plastic beakers! Norma I want Rodney to try this King of kings wine! Hang on I'll nip back to my car." She turned and went out leaving Norma holding the Barolo and Rodney gob smacked.

Julia returned carrying a picnic hamper which she dually opened and produced four large goblets and a checked tablecloth. "Come on Norma, haven't you got a table and some chairs back there," she nodded her head at the door of the back of the shop. Rodney was about to protest and Julia seeing this beamed at him and said "You know Rodney, Norma's told us so much about you and your expert knowledge and love of cheeses! That Mr Ullivari really would like us to try some next Friday. He'd like us to do a blind tasting of English and Italian cheeses, to guess which is which, and to say which is the strongest, smoothest, creamiest etcetera…..Oh! I think Norma would really enjoy that Wouldn't you Norma?" Norma gasped; Julia was like a whirl wind, before she knew it the old chairs and table were in the front of the shop with the tablecloth spread out and the glasses, wine and three plates.

Julia sat down and patted another chair, "Come on Rodney! Let your customers see you trying the king of wine with the king of English cheese---bring on the Blacksticks!"

Norma watched as Rodney sat down and cut into his favourite cheese and placed around a dozen cubes on a plate. She watched as Julia coaxed him into taking a sip of Barolo. Her dour Rodney, who knew what he liked and who was so set in his ways, was being led to the Barolo like a lamb to the slaughter. Norma smiled, a grin of sheer delight "I know you'll like it love 'cause I like it…I think it's pure nectar!"

Rodney turned to Norma, and it was then that Julia saw this dour mans expressionless face change from stone like impassiveness to a look of tenderness and joy. "You know I know what I like Norma, but for you love I'll do anything, especially if it makes you happy!"

With that he raised his goblet and took a draft of the sweet wine, he kept the wine in his mouth and rolled it round, tasting it as it slowly warmed his throat- he even closed his eyes. After what seemed an age he looked up, nodded his head and said "You know what Norma, you were right, it's pure nectar, and it'll go lovely with the Blacksticks."

Rodney was undemonstrative, like many northern men of his age, he was also a man of few words, but for all that Julia had realized that these two cheese lovers were not boring; just gentle innocents moving into old age with an understanding of each other's needs that far outweighed any sexual passionate young love.

Norma came and sat next to Rodney and sipped a little of the Barolo and ate a small cube of the Blacksticks. She moved closer to Rodney and squeezed his hand. "I knew you'd like it… I've been trying to tell you for such a long time… Wine goes real well with cheese and I'd like to try to get a licence to sell wines." "Steady on there… this is Best wood love… There's no call for posh drinks here! You can enjoy your wine with the ladies, I'll even let you take some of my cheeses, but let's not be hasty, all right love!" Rodney had been drawn as far as he'd go for now.

So Julia would call for Norma the following Friday and they would bring a tray of Rodney's cheeses all neatly labelled and lovingly described by Rodney. Rodney himself would decline the idea of a cheese tasting and competition, Norma would do the honours, as Rodney felt sure she knew as much as he did, and she'd enjoy it much more. "Ah well" said Norma "You can take a horse to water but you can't make it drink! And my Rodney can be real stubborn, I told you, he's set in his ways. I wish he'd trust me and let me introduce a few things. But Julia you've done wonders this morning....I've never seen Rodney drink wine before! Mind you that Barolo is lovely.... I'll give him a sip at bedtime, you never know, it might win him over!"

Chapter Twelve..

In Cheese We Trust.

Rodney got the trays ready for Norma and he helped her prepare a little talk on the qualities of a good Lancashire cheese. He did taste the Barolo on a number of evenings and he did confess to Norma that it was much better than the pint of pale ale he had at the golf club on Saturdays after their game of golf. It still wasn't as good as a nice cup of tea though! "Oh! Rodney! What am I going to do with you?" laughed Norma "You can still have tea and teacakes as well as wine and cheese… Oh look here's Julia come for me….are you sure you won't come love…the ladies are ever so nice, they won't eat you, only your cheese!"

Julia tried to coax Rodney too, but he was adamant that Norma was much better in company than he was; besides he'd like to just sit nice and quiet with his book… he felt a bit tired as well, he might even have an early night. He gave Norma an affectionate peak on the cheek and helped her on with her coat and waved her off from the front door.

"You can't win him over love… so don't fret, he's happy at home. As snug as a bug in a rug; he'll read his book, have a cup of cocoa at 9 o'clock and be fast asleep in bed by 10.30". Norma sighed deeply and folded her arms and smiled, she knew her Rodney. He was set in his ways.

Antonio helped Norma set out her trays of cheese, and introduced her to Mr Carlo Poncepé. He was a short but rotund, bolding, Italian, elderly gentleman with a large moustache and sideburns. He grinned and made a very friendly welcoming embrace to Norma, who responded in bemused and embarrassed confusion. "I think you and I are going to have a cheese tasting and a competition Yes? I've brought plenty cheese, plenty olives, plenty anti pasta, but most of all - cause Antonio say you like it - plenty Barolo and plenty wine!"

60

"Oh! Mr Carlo! Please it's not just me who's going to taste the cheese it's all the ladies…but I must admit I do like your Barolo and my Rodney does too!"

"Yes! But first we have to be very sensible and pretend we like all this art and beauty, we must be clever and cultured…. So you sit by me Norma and we sip wine and nod and say *bene bene* O.K.!"

Norma smiled gently "Well Mr Carlo I   must admit all this art and culture and that sort of thing, well it leaves me cold… Suppose it's 'cause I'm too simple to understand it!" "Me too! I just like to enjoy good food and wine, as my belly shows everyone." And Carlo laughed and patted his corpulent tummy.

The group of ladies gathered round the large screen and viewed a large copy of Titians Venus of Urbino "There is something deliciously erotic about this beautiful aristocratic nude lady, there she is staring out at you, daring you to be shocked, she is poised, so relaxed on her couch in her nudity, she is self-assured and confident her body needs no adornment, she is seductively naked.". "Strange how paintings over three hundred years old can still present the viewer with a feeling of unease, as if one is being challenged in some way; it's as if she is daring you to be shocked! I know it's technically clever and beautiful, but I find it very provocative." This was Julia enjoying art and thinking aloud.. "Oh! You're on a higher plain than me! I just think she's saying come on take me! Take me! Take me if you dare! "Vittorio was lusting after his women again "I love women they are beautiful, sublime, a wonderful creation God gave to man to enjoy and so I enjoy, I enjoy!"

"And don't we know it!" said Tanya and gave him a playful slap on his shoulder. Vittorio winced and continued "You must enjoy life; you have to grab life by the balls, before it leaves you, that's all I think you can do, don't hurt anyone but enjoy everyone yes?" Vittorio grasped Ella who was sitting next to him and planted a lusty kiss on her cleavage! Ella pushed his head gently away and said "down boy! Leave my balls alone!... Come along Norma and Carlo introduce us to something with a bit of taste and a lot of clout and a strong bite!"

Norma laughed as did Carlo and everyone else even Vittorio "Oh you are naughty but very nice." Said Norma, and rose to the occasion with Carlo. She talked of the many lovely local cheeses that were to be found in and around Lancashire, how many had almost been lost to the public with the development of supermarkets and big dairy outlets. She told how her Rodney had travelled round to small farms, and tried to bring back some of the local tasty cheeses and bring them to the attention of local people. Rodney was really only interested in Lancashire cheeses, from the mild and creamy soft, to the tangy strong crumbly, from the kick of a powerful Lancashire bomb to the true bite of a ridge making Blackstick. Rodney knew his Lancashire cheeses, they were his passion and his pleasure, and he hoped the ladies would enjoy them too.

Everyone tasted just a morsel of each, even Carlo. Carlo was a true Italian gentleman in every sense, he praised Norma handsomely and her cheeses too! He politely asked if he could give a little description of some of the cheeses he had selected for the ladies to try. He described the different areas the cheeses came from, and how the villagers were fiercely protective of their cheeses refusing to try any foreign variety (how like Rodney they were).

There followed a good hour of comparing and contrasting cheese after cheese, taste after taste, and always with just a sip of the Barolo. The evening was speeding by, and Norma was mellowing like her cheese and getting quietly sloshed (only mildly) with Barolo.

Mr Poncepé was evidently in his element, enjoying giving these ladies the chance to taste some unfamiliar and unforgettable cheeses. Eventually a vote was taken and the Gorgonzola was declared the strongest cheese, but the Blacksticks had a more winnable bite (and went better with the Barolo, Norma declared).

It had been a very convivial evening and all had enjoyed it. Tracey had left with Toni, taking a small selection of all the cheeses. Ella had left with Karen McNaulty the Lady captain of Whittley Green, again with a selection of cheeses, but these were for the golf club, Ella couldn't have cheese … it went straight to her boobs.

Norma left with Mr Poncepé he said "I take this queen of cheese home! With another bottle of my king of wines. You are a great lady and I'd like to meet with Rodney, to discuss cheeses!"

He put Norma's trays into the back of his van, and he told everyone they must arrange for another great evening like this, it was *multo bene, multo bene*!

Norma left all smiles, in fact a very big cheesy grin… she'd really! Really! Enjoyed this evening. Mr Carlo was a true gentleman and she was sure Rodney would get on well with him; they'd enjoy talking cheeses, perhaps Mr Carlo could talk to him about wine as well.

She was telling Carlo all about her dreams and ambitions for the cheese shop (the Barolo had given Norma the courage to express her real longings to expand the business) and he was nodding and approving her ideas, even suggesting she might do cheese tastings in the shop. He'd like to be her wine supplier, if she got a licence that is. Norma then explained to Carlo that her Rodney was a very cautious Northern gentleman, very set in his ways. He never did anything hasty, and he'd felt there was no call for posh drinks in Bestwood, and Norma would always be guided by Rodney,

"Cause we're a team and I always do what Rodney wants, we're happy that way."

"Well let me talk to Rodney... I think I can make him an offer he'd be happy with, and it would fit in with your ambitions, see, we talk over cheese.... And a glass of *Barolo*."

Mr Poncepé asked directions, for Bestwood was well into the hills, and the lanes twisted and turned dizzily in these northern climbs. "Well if you look over there to your left you can see Bestwood down there, it was once a thriving mining town, busy, bustling and cheerful, but that was before M.T. And we don't talk about that."

Carlo looked quizzical "M.T. I don't know this, what is it?" Norma sniffed and in a hushed voice whispered "Margret Thatcher... her and her cronies shut the mine, and closed the industry down, the town sort of died, it never really recovered. It took its heart when they closed the mine. Rodney says he can see how men feel useless and lose their dignity, and even their will to live..... He never felt that. We've always had the shop and each other, that's enough for us!"

Carlo realized that Rodney's decisions would be the final word for Norma, but he felt sure if he could talk to this man he'd strike a bond. They pulled up outside the neat old stone built cottage, there was a light on downstairs.. "Oh Rodney's still up, may be you can have a chat after all."

They found Rodney, a smile on his face, his eyes closed and a sherry glass of Barolo in his hand, a picture of contentment. He was still warm, but not asleep. Rodney ,bless him, had had a massive heart attack, they said at the post mortem, it must have just happened a few minutes before Norma's return.

Norma was distraught and poor Mr Poncepé desperately anxious to find help rang Antonio, who rang Julia. They had all arrived at the cottage as the ambulance arrived. Norma held Rodney's head in her arms and sobbed as she rocked him to and fro "Oh Rodney don't leave me love, don't leave me, what ever shall I do without you!..Oh! Come on love! Wake up, please! Please wake up!"

The paramedics were wonderfully tender, gentle and consoling. Gently persuading Norma to release Rodney, and checking for any sign of a heart beat… there was none, and yet they still tried, poor, poor Rodney, Poor, poor Norma. She was like a bewildered lost child, sobbing and wondering round and round the little living room wringing her hands, and then - begging the ambulance men "Wake him up! Please wake him up!"

Antonio Ullivari took her by the hands and held her to his chest "You know, you have to let the ambulance men take him Norma! The doctor, he's coming and you have to let them take him Norma. I'm sorry but you have to do this."

Norma gave in at this point, she just sank into a well of grief, unable to speak only her heart rending sobs passed her lips. The doctor arrived and looked quickly at Rodney and whispered D.O.A. and moved to Norma, he held her hand and told her "You know Mrs Gibson there's nothing we can do, is there anyone we can contact to stay with you?" Norma wailed and shook her head "There's only me and Rodney." Julia bent down beside Norma and placed her hand on Norma's shoulder "No, Norma you're not alone there are your friends, and I'll look after you now, you'll come home with me, James won't mind."

Norma left with Julia; Rodney was taken to the hospital mortuary (an autopsy would have to take place, as it was a sudden death.) Antonio Ullivari and Carlo Poncepé closed the cottage and took the keys. They would organize the funeral and make arrangements for Norma….she was truly a golf widow now.

Chapter Thirteen.

An Italian ladies Society Organize A Very Northern Funeral.

Julia took Norma home, where James seemed genuinely shocked and sorry for Norma. He gave her a good stiff brandy and ensured that she would sleep for a few hours. He'd contact her doctor and speak to Giles Smythe –Dawson; he'd know what to do. But for now Norma must be given a chance to get over the shock. "Yes I'll sleep in the chair near her, I don't want her being alone and to be upset when she wakes." Said Julia, and with that the few hours of night fall left, were given over to fretful and heart aching sleep. A product of emotional exhaustion and the bitterness of grief.

Antonio Ullivari phoned all the ladies of the Italian Society the next morning and gave them the heart rending news. Every one of the ladies responded the same way, they would go to Norma immediately. They would support her and try to ease the unbearable pain they knew Norma would feel.

Norma was drowning or so she felt, submerged in a world of confusion and pain, her brain and heart unable to control the surges of anguish that overtook her. She'd been with Rodney for over forty years and it wasn't right that he wasn't there anymore. She couldn't think, couldn't cope and didn't want to live now. Feeling this way, she left everything to Julia and the Italian Ladies Society—It didn't matter anymore, Rodney wasn't there to say whether it was right or wrong.

James rang Norma's doctor who said he would call later that day, there was little to be done however as no autopsy would take place until Monday. "God how insensitive of him, I can't tell Norma that!" James was at a loss to know what to do, when the doorbell rang, he answered it to find a company of ladies and Carlo Poncepé looking so forlorn, waiting to speak and comfort Norma.

He took Norma's hands in his and in a sobbing voice begged Norma's forgiveness. "If I hadn't talked so much we might have arrived earlier—I'm so sorry. Oh! Forgive me please!" he broke down and sobbed.

This gave Norma the excuse to sob as well and to accept the sympathy and support that the ladies began to give. "You know Mr Carlo, it wasn't anyone's fault, and my Rodney always did things on his own, in his own way. He was set in his ways, God love him he even chose to die without fuss!" and Norma sighed such a heavy sigh.

Julia brought in a tray with tea and biscuits, asking everyone to help themselves. Tracey persuaded Norma to have some tea. She looked sympathetically at Norma and realized that Norma was old enough to be her mother. A wave of feminine emotion swept over her, putting her arms round Norma she told her "You'll be a mum to me Norma 'cause mine died before I knew her. I know I can't replace Rodney but I do care about you!"

It was Karen McNaulty who offered calm advice, she asked if Norma was a church goer, and if so would she like her to ring the vicar. Ms McNaulty the lady captain at Whiteley Green was a marvellous organizer and had a calm cool head on her. She was a strong leader and a professional lawyer who was used to being in charge. The Methodist minister was contacted, and before the ladies had finished their tea, she arrived. A charming lady minister, who offered sympathy, advice and practical funeral arrangements. There would be a service at the little Methodist chapel, where Rodney and Norma had married over forty years ago; it would be followed by a cremation. Ms Mcnaulty suggested she make arrangements for a light luncheon at the golf club in honour of Rodney's memory. Norma was so grateful that all this organizing was taken out of her hands. A kind of numb calmness came over her. She sighed a lot, but somehow the aching in her heart was lulled. She thanked Julia "it's very kind and good of you, but I must get back home, I need to take stock, think a little, and try to sort things out." Tanya knelt by Norma's chair and suggested "why don't I come with you Norma, I've handled a few funerals and insurance arrangements at the office in my time, so I know what needs to be done." Norma took Tanya's hand and kissed it and tearfully said "You're all being so kind, I don't know how I'll manage without your help, thank you all of you!"

Carlo Poncepé asked Norma "Would it be alright if I closed the cheese shop for you for a few days? .. I can do that for Rodney, Yes?" Everything was coming to a close; with Norma's return to the cottage and with Tanya's help Rodney's affairs were put in order.

On the following Tuesday the ladies society met and discussed the arrangements for the funeral. Vittorio Tartaglioni would be returning to Firenze after the funeral to his marble quarry and studio. He would personally make two marble pillars with Greek urns and inscriptions "In loving memory of Rodney Gibson 1942-2010 A loving husband a contented man and a happy golfer." One would be placed in Norma's garden and the other at the entrance of Whittley Greens 18th hole. Antonio Ullivari would arrange the music and requiem. Julia would read the eulogy. Tracey, Toni and Karen McNaulty would provide the luncheon and Carlo Poncepé would provide a dozen bottles of Barolo. Ella and Giles Smythe- Dawson would accompany Norma from her home to the church and the crematorium; she would not be alone.

Norma was weeping softly as these arrangements were finalized, but she smiled through her tears and gave a kind of strangled chuckle…"Aye! Wouldn't my Rodney have enjoyed this- he'd have said they've done me proud love! A right proper send off. I couldn't have organized it any better me self!"

A little over a week later in the small Methodist Chapel at Bestwood, on a bright sunny day, Norma Gibson and the Ladies Italian Society and some of Whittley Greens Golfers came to celebrate the life of a very ordinary Northern gentleman. He was set in his ways, but big in his heart, as Norma wrote in his eulogy.

Julia came in front of the little congregation, in a neat black suit, she didn't wear a hat. She read from the dais. The chapel was a small, plain and simple chapel, but it carried Julia's gentle voice clearly. "Norma has asked me to read the eulogy she wrote for her Rodney. She feels emotionally unable to read her thoughts out today, but she wishes me to convey her grateful thanks to you all for your kindness and support. Norma wrote in praise of Rodney.

I've known him most of my life

He was always kind of gentle

Soft spoken, shy, not pushy

Just very set in his ways.

He weren't showy or brash or soppy;

But for all of his dour ways,

I knew that he really loved me

He showed that in his plain simple ways.

Oh Rodney how I'll miss you,

How I'll long for your soft embrace,

Of an evening, I'll miss you say

Hutch up to my breast love

T'is the end of a beautiful day.

Norma cried softly and was comforted by a weeping Tracey, who in turn was comforted by Toni who held her gently and kissed her cheek and wiped her tears away.

It was a very moving service, yet it was with dignity, "not over the top" as Rodney would say. Rodney's funeral moved on to its inevitable conclusion, until all farewells were said. Norma returned home to her empty cottage, to mourn for Rodney, while sipping a glass of Barolo and nibbling some strong tangy Blacksticks with a slice of Lancashire crumbly too, yes, her dear Rodney was very set in his ways.

In the weeks that were to follow Norma had frequent visitors, Tanya came to sort out Rodney's insurance and to give advice on gaining a licence for the shop. Mr Poncepé came and helped to keep the shop ticking over. Giles Smythe-Dawson was dragged round by Ella to sort out Rodney's probate. He didn't want to be involved, but if Ella insisted he'd do it, it might help him get votes for the captaincy.

Tracey didn't come and Norma wondered why? She'd have to phone her, it wasn't like Tracey to not get in touch.

Chapter Fourteen

Tracey and Toni Reap Jasons Wrath.

Jason Doupé went to Rodney's funeral because James, Mark and Giles were going. He'd tagged along to keep in with the group, but really, Rodney Gibson was an old maid and nobody gave him a seconds notice. He was therefore quite surprised at the turn out and at the emotional response of some of the mourners.

The eulogy that Julia so movingly red, caused an overwhelming response from Norma's friends, especially Tracey, she had sobbed out loud as had Norma. Jason began to feel embarrassed at this display of raw emotion, but his embarrassment turned to real anger as he watched Toni put her arms round Tracey and kiss the tears away.

That ugly Italian cow was being a mite too supportive of his wife! Jason became puce with rage, he was seething with anger. That little Italian chef was obviously more than just a friend. She was an evil bitch, who had stolen his frigid useless wife from under his nose; the filthy Italian lesbian.

All through the rest of the funeral arrangements Jason seethed and breathed heavily, it was hard containing his anger, indeed it festered as he watched the two women in their grief. By the time of the funeral luncheon his nostrils were flaring, his face puce, he sidled up to Tracey in the golf club lounge. He gripped her round the waist and pulled her towards him, and then in the deadliest menacing whisper, he taunted her. "You filthy whore, you fucking lesbian, come on it's time for my little wifey to come home!" Tracey couldn't protest, not here at Rodney's funeral in front of a grieving Norma, but her eyes met Toni's and conveyed all the terror she was feeling.

Jason pulled Tracey even closer to his chest and forcibly marched her quickly out dragging her to his waiting

Merc. He punched her into the front seat and 'child locked' the door.

What later followed at the family home was bestial in the extreme. Jason smashed Tracey against the hall wall pushing her face hard into it."So you like it from behind do you! Whore, bitch…did she do this then!" Jason was roaring like a wild bull, his face now crimson, his eyes wild, spit dribbling from his mouth. He tore at Tracey's clothes, grasping her pubic hair and wrenching it, thrusting his hands into her virginal flesh.

Then, testosterone flowing madly, he mounted her raping and buggering her again and again and again, all the time roaring like a demented wild animal. Tracey's screams only seemed to exhilarate and invigorate him like an exalting bull. Jason had become a demonic male, he dragged Tracey up the stairs and threw her into the bedroom locking the door, and she was a prisoner in her own home.

She lay there like a damaged mauled deer, she could feel her own blood trickling down her legs, her face was already swelling from its repeated crashing against the wall. Her mind blanked at this point and she fainted into a kind of oblivion.

Demonic and exhilarated with his testosterone-fed anger, Jason waited for Toni's return to the house, he sat in the darkened hall, very still, with only the sound of his breathing, heavy, menacing, he waited for his prey.

He found Tracey's mobile lying at the foot of the stairs. A smile of sheer malice spread across his face, it was so easy, he found Toni's number and texted just two words, help me, and waited.

Toni, who had seen the fear in Tracey's eyes as she left the funeral luncheon, was already alarmed and worried, but, when she received the text, she knew she had to leave. She came to Norma and in very broken English begged to leave saying "We come see you very soon, so very sorry." She kissed Norma and wept; Norma smiled through her tears and said "I know I'll see you both soon."

Toni left running to her little mini, she had to get to Tracey as fast as possible. She drove madly, fast and furious, only to find the house in ominous darkness. She fumbled blindly in her bag for the front door key and struggled to unlock the door. It was dark as she entered and she called "Tracey, Tracey, I come" but she got no further, Jason leapt onto her back and slammed her head against the same wall he had attacked Tracey on.

Toni gasped as the air was knocked out of her. She fought for breath, trying to free herself from this bestial bear lock she was held in. Toni had suffered much abuse from her Sicilian father, she had seen him sadistically force her mother to have sex in front of his children, but what she was about to endure was far worse.

Jason was like a rampant lion as he roared in her ears "You filthy fucking lesbian whore, I'll show you what it's really like to fuck" and he tore into her very entrails, sodomizing her with his Testosterone swollen penis, he shouted in her ears, "This is where you don't put it right--- but for a bitch like you- feel it! "And he thrust himself in her, pushing her hard against the wall. Toni screamed with pain and tried to escape, which only produced an even more violent reaction from Jason. "You want it again little Itie" and he thrust and squirmed bouncing her body again and again against the wall. "No, please God no!" she screamed. Jason grabbed her beautiful chestnut hair and pulled her over to the telephone chair, he pushed her over it. She clawed and scratched at his face. He bit her in response and then, he mounted her like a Bull Elephant crashing into her virginity, flooding her with his anger induced sperm. She screamed as he yelled and bellowed "Yes! Cow have it…have it! "She scratched his face again, and he hit her! Then all Testosterone

73

spent her threw her on the floor. "Don't be here when I get back" he screamed. He threw her small bag of belongings down the stairs. "Tracey doesn't need you so clear out bitch!" Jason stormed out of the house slamming the door, leaving Toni lying face down in a pool of sperm and blood. She crawled to the door dragging her belongings, and now sobbing uncontrollably she fled from Tracey's home, she didn't know where, so she drove and drove, anywhere, to escape from what had just taken place.

Tracey lay on the floor of the bedroom unconscious as to what had happened, her own body bruised and aching from the assault made upon it. It was some time later that evening she finally surfaced from oblivion, only to sob with horror at the realization of what had occurred.

She didn't know what had happened to Toni, she only knew what had been forced upon her. She tried to stand, but felt to sore and weak, so she crawled to the bed and fell back into sub-consciousness. She was drifting in and out of a nightmarish world where Jason's penis was endlessly coming towards her and far in the distance Toni beckoning. Tracey awoke again, it was night, and she stumbled to the bathroom. Filling the bath, with warm, fragrant, soapy water and laying in it gently rubbing her defiled mound of Venus. She was trapped, she was Jason's object of derision, to be used and abused as he saw fit. Tracey wished she was dead.

When Jason returned he was ruthlessly calm. He looked at her and smirked. "Well you'll be house bound now for at least a week. Oh! By the way that little Italian bitch won't be coming here again, so you'll get all the rest you need!"

So Tracey in painful isolation tried to recover from her terrible sexual ordeal. Jason left her completely alone, but locked in her bedroom. He answered the phone and explained to Julia, Tracey wouldn't be coming to their little club anymore, and she was finding it to upsetting.

Chapter Fifteen.
Tracey and Toni Find Safety and Sanctuary.

Julia was worried; Norma felt there was something wrong, why Toni and Tracey hadn't rung at least, even if they couldn't visit. Julia asked Antonio if he knew why the two women were so quiet. It was then that all the ladies who do knew something was amiss.

Antonio had received a telephone call from the Little Sisters of Mercy, a convent, informing him that Miss Boghini was receiving sanctuary, solace and spiritual comfort; she would return when she was physically, mentally and spiritually better able to cope.

All the ladies sat together discussing this information, and putting two and two together, they had come to the conclusion that something was most definitely wrong. Ella suggested that she call round to see Tracey and make arrangements to play some golf. Jason surely couldn't say that was upsetting. Karen McNaulty said she would write a letter as the lady captain requesting Tracey fill in the competition form for the ladies doubles, if there was no reply then Ella could quite reasonably call. This was agreed although Tanya felt too much time was being taken and that she might call round anyway. But Ms McNaulty protested "No don't do that please! Be very careful of Mr Doupé, he's a man with a velvet tongue, but I think he's a bit of a control freak and might be quite deranged if you challenge him!"

Karen McNaulty was a civil and family law practitioner as well as the Lady Captain. She was a cool headed, perceptive lawyer and she also had a ruthless streak in her that helped when she quietly and coldly cross examined claimants. She would smile brightly in their face as she gently stabbed them in the back with her pointed questions.

She had summed Jason Doupé up in the few rounds of golf she had had to play with him. He was arrogant, domineering and easily lost his temper. He had displayed this uncontrollable rage on a few occasions at Whittley Green, but never quite enough to gain a warning from the stewards.

The following week the golf competition form was sent, but no reply was received and so Ella Smythe- Dawson was given the go ahead to call on Tracey Doupé.

A month had passed since Rodney's death and life was blossoming on the golf course. Ella was becoming a very proficient golfer and Todd enjoyed playing with her, their rounds of golf were fun too! Ella made arrangements to have early morning practice rounds with him, before the course had anyone else on, she was, he said, becoming some super swinging lady golfer and her assets weren't getting in the way either.

Giles was still unaware of Ella's' new found talent, although he had heard a rumour about some super woman who was rivalling the men with her super swing. He was however to busy sowing brownie points towards the captaincy to listen to gossip of that sort. So Giles blissfully unaware of Ella's golfing expeditions, left her able to call round to the Doupés home on the following Friday.

Jason Doupé although worried and guilt ridden about his actions after the funeral, was still keeping Tracey a prisoner in her own home. He had removed all means of communication and locked her in her own bedroom. He had told Jason Junior that his mother was suffering from acute nervous exhaustion and she should not be disturbed by anyone, not even himself.

When Ella arrived on the doorstep at 8.15am Jason Junior answered, he was quite overawed by this rather gorgeous lady and her beautiful big hazel eyes, lushes lips and fantastic tits, wow! Ella smiled and fluttered her lashes "Oh you must be Jason Junior, your mum's told me so much about you, I've come for our practise round of golf...is she ready?" and with that Ella stepped into the hall; Jason was all confused. He tried desperately to say what his father had told him, but somehow it didn't ring true. Ella just looked at him as if he were a chicken about to lay a square egg. "Oh! Come on darling, this is me, Ella Smythe- Dawson, your mums secret golf partner, just tell your dad to come and find us on the golf course if he's that worried about her! Come on take me to her."

Jason felt he had no option, so he led Ella upstairs and unlocked the bedroom door. He was visibly shocked when he saw Tracey, she was still baring bruises round her face and she was very weak and thin Ella was equally shocked but masked it well. She took one look at Tracey and said "come on girl, get dressed we've an appointment with the pro at 10 o'clock so chop-chop sweetie!"

"Buzz off Jason darling! Your mum can't get dressed while you're in the room!"

Tracey was hustled into trousers and a fleecy, golf shoes and a headscarf over her hair. Ella bustled her quickly out and into her waiting car. She turned to Jason Junior and said "Tell your dad we're on the golf course with Todd the pro and Karen McNaulty the Lady Captain, we'll bring her back later. Bye...mission accomplished with minimum stress let's get out of here PDQ" whispered Ella and Tracey sobbed with relief.

At the golf course Karen McNaulty was waiting in the Lady Captain's room with Julia and Tanya. Ella had warned them on her mobile that Tracey was in need of help. When they saw Tracey they too were shocked, but it was Ms McNaulty whose gentle questions probed and delved and finally revealed the true horror of that day. Tracey confessed to her love of Toni and to her feelings of guilt, she was almost taking the blame for Jason's inhuman behaviour, Ms McNaulty calmly smiled at her and told her that Ms Boghini was at this time in the Little Sisters of Mercy convent, receiving sanctuary, solace and medical attention, the nature of which they didn't know, but had a good idea it bore a similar resemblance to Tracey's own.

Tracey was beside herself with fear and worry, she must find out how Toni was and what had happened to her, what could they do? Ms McNaulty suggested breakfast might help and Tracey reluctantly agreed. Over coffee and croissants they phoned Norma, who promptly closed the cheese shop and made Carlo take her to the convent to collect Toni.

After breakfast, Ella, Karen and Tracey set off with Todd round the golf course, they had reached the 11th green when they saw Jason Doupé coming over the horizon towards them, anger and defiance written all over his face. "What the hell are you doing with my!" but Ella coolly cut his outburst off "Oh! Hi! Jason, well I suppose we'll have to let you into our little secret…so long as you don't tell Giles! Tracey and I have been taking secret golf lessons and we've entered the ladies doubles competition, so we just have to practise as much as possible." Jason glared at Tracey and then at Ella. He was trying to work out how much Tracey had said and how much they all knew.

Karen McNaulty smiled sweetly at Jason "Why Jason your concern for Tracey's well-being is commendable, but I think we ladies understand women's problems far better than you men! And we are going to keep a careful and watchful eye over her… to ensure she is in perfect healthy condition for the coming competitions. I'm quite sure you'll be relieved that we'll look after Tracey…Yes?"

Jason didn't know what to say, he was obviously made aware that Ms McNaulty and Ella knew everything, he couldn't call their bluff, he had to accept their terms or risk further disclosures of his bestial sexual behaviour.

"So if it's O.K. with you Jason, Trace and I will be round the golf course every morning at 8.30 and Giles will never know anything!... and it'll be a super! Super surprise on captains day...you can keep mum about it can't you? If you know what I mean?" Ella put a protective arm around Tracey, and Jason knew exactly what she meant. He looked sheepish, and defeated, he muttered as he walked away "bloody women!" "It's alright Jason I'll bring her back later today, we're going to have lunch at Penguinos...Tracey feels peckish and wants to see Norma and the girls, don't you darling? Now remember Jason no giving our little secret away O.K.!" Ella and Karen burst out laughing and Todd Hornermann threw in for good measure "I know Jason won't say a word to ruin you ladies and your chances of being prize winners on captain's day!"

Jason Doupé walked off the golf course and back to his large maroon Mercedes, his tail down and well between his legs.

Chapter Sixteen.

Norma Offers Protection After Toni's Revolation.

Norma and Carlo Poncepé arrived at the convent and were taken to see the Mother Superior. She seemed quite reluctant at first to allow them to see Toni; she explained "Ms Boghini is in a very sensitive and fragile state, we have nursed her these past few weeks, and little by little she has revealed what has happened to her, I can't tell you what she has suffered and what she has confessed to. But I will ask Toni if she will see you? Please wait here."

It seemed like an age had passed as they waited and waited. Carlo rubbing his large moustache and sighing, but when Toni entered it was Norma who gasped, stood up and rushed to her and put her arms round her, "Oh! My little love whatever's happened to you?" This truly maternal caring was too much for Toni and she broke down and retold the events of the funeral evening. Norma rocked to and fro in shock and distress, but Carlo started sobbing and speaking in his husky Italian said "My God Toni! You come with me, I mean us, Norma and I, we'll look after you, we'll take care of you, you are a victim woman! A victim!"

Toni rocked to and fro like Norma, and began sobbing uncontrollably she wailed in Italian "No don't you see it's not just what he did to me! It's left me feeling dirty, defiled and..(Here she paused and wiped the tears away, she gave an agonizing sob) Oh! God Forgive me, he's made me pregnant!"

Carlo collapsed with shock into his chair, he began to wail as well, and Norma desperately asked him to tell her what Toni had said. It was a good few moments before he managed to compose himself, then breathing deeply the old man rose, he put his big arms round Toni's bowed shoulders, and very quietly described what had happened to Toni. As he wiped away his own tears, he said "Because of this rape! This girl is now with child!" Norma gasped and put her arms round Toni too, she hugged her to her breast and said "Come home love, my house is empty I'll look after you, I'll look after you as if you were my own! Carlo get Toni's things we're taking our girl home!"

So barely six weeks after Rodney's demise and Norma's heart aching grief, her home was to become a safe haven, a sanctuary for Toni. Norma was like a mother hen, feathering her nest, busy caring for Toni, she had a reason to live again, and the cottage would be a home once more.

They took Toni to Penguinos where Julia, Tanya and Antonio Ullivari were waiting. Norma sat down with Toni and insisted that she have a good pasta lunch immediately. The ladies all sat and ate and waited to hear what had happened.

While they sat eating, Carlo took Antonio to one side and told him what had happened to Toni. Antonio went cold with anger, he wanted to arrange for some Florentine justice, and he wanted his waiters to administer it in the Sicilian fashion. Carlo then told him Toni was, through the rape, pregnant. Antonio couldn't help crying out in anger "God! No, Oh! no!"

They were all horrified; ready to committee some terrible revenge on Jason Doupé for what he had inflicted on their Toni. The door opened at that moment and Ella, Karen McNaulty and Tracey walked in. They saw Norma fussing and caring for Toni. Antonio came over to Tracey, he was about to tell her the news of Toni, when Toni herself blurted out her condition. She grasped Tracey's hand and kissed it. Then turning to Antonio she said in Italian "What's done is done, and we have to live with it.I can't take away this life that's been forced on me, neither can I deny the feelings I have for Tracey, God forgive me, but I fear for her more than myself, Jason Doupé is her husband after all."

Tracey sobbed; Ella shook her head in disbelief and said "Don't you worry about Tracey, Honey, Karen and I have got that bastard mastered. In fact Karen is writing up a legal document for Tracey and we're going to get Jason to sign it; but that doesn't help you and your condition."

"She's coming to live with me…me and Mr Carlo we'll look after her; we'll see her right…and the baby. So don't you worry about Toni, just get that evil monster off our girls, that's what I want...Carlo pour me a *Barolo*…I need it!"Exclaimed the normally placid lady.

Antonio Ullivari was still seething; he couldn't understand these two women, why were they not seeking revenge? Why were they almost taking the blame for Jason's brutal behaviour? Then he recalled his own wife's detestation and abhorrence of sex and men in general. Any attempts were met with total rejection and therefore Antonio gave up their relationship. "I hope you don't think all men are like this? Tracey, Toni, we aren't animals, we can be kind, we are capable of love. You two have had a terrible experience and a rotten deal in life and I'm truly sorry for you, I'd seek revenge, but then you're the gentler sex!"

Toni smiled through her tears and said to Antonio "I'll be back in the kitchen if you'll have me that is? I'm going to live with Norma, so I'll be well looked after. I'm safe and strong, I can manage, I just want to be sure that Tracey is safe."

Ms McNaulty took out a large A4 document and handed it over to Tracey, it read like a court order, a restraining order to one Jason Doupe, he was to have no contact with Tracey Doupe or any visiting rights to her abode or place of work. Ms McNaulty looked kindly at Tracey and said "All we have to do is get him to sign it, but leave that problem with me and Ella. I'll see you tomorrow on the golf course! I think we're going to have to enter the mixed doubles competition, it's a pity Julia and Tanya don't play golf too!"

"Oh don't even suggest it! Golf has caused enough trouble in our lives as it is, that's why we set up the Ladies Italian Society in the first place!" Tanya raised her glass of Barolo and grinning at the ladies said "here's to our society, and to the ladies mixed doubles competition and may the ladies win!"

Chapter Seventeen.

Preparing For The Ladies Mixed Doubles Competition.

Ella was as good as her word, she arrived at 8 o'clock and called for Tracey, who was up dressed and waiting. "Jason left the house this morning he said he was going to a Mercedes exhibition, and he'd be away for a couple of days, but he'd sort me out when he's back!" Ella grinned "Good that gives us a few days to get things arranged on the golf course. Does he have an E mail address?"

Tracey wrote it down and gave it to Ella, she was trying to be as positive as Ella was, but it was bloody hard and she was petrified of Jason.

Half an hour later , on the third green, Karen McNaulty showed how her reputation as an excellent divorce settlement lawyer was well earned. She would personally contact Mr Doupe and outline the alternatives of what would happen if he decided not to sign and abide by the restraining order; she would relish taking court action. Of course that would mean getting the police and the crown prosecution service involved for rape and physical violence on Ms Burghini that would naturally follow; there was ample evidence both of a photographic and D.N.A. material. Yes, Ms McNaulty was not a Q.C. for her gentle nature, she was, as most defence barristers knew to their cost, a needle sharp piercing advocate and usually got the settlements her clients required. Her reputation as the leading divorce lawyer was widespread and her chambers was the best in the North West for resolving alimony and matrimonial separations for the deeply Catholic communities of Irish and Italian decent. Karen quietly assured Tracey that she wouldn't have to endure Jason's presence anymore. If she required any further assistance of a legal nature she would in this case defer any fees and ask for costs to be taken into account on the settlement in court. Jason Doupe would be well and truly screwed, his reputation in tatters and his financial wellbeing castrated, he would Ms McNaulty said "be well and truly fucked up!" and with that she swung her driver hard and the ball flew high overhead and landed on the edge of the green. Karen McNaulty smiled, satisfied that she was an excellent golfer, as well as a leading family law barrister.

Tracey was to some degree reassured and mollified, and Ella said "look Tracey you're under my protection, Giles thinks I'm doing this for you; I am in away, but he'll learn, come the mixed doubles competition, you're going to partner him!" Ms McNaulty nodded and laughed as she said "and guess who's partnering Jason! Yes me… and I can't wait. I've sent Mr Doupe a few interesting Emails as yet there's been no response but we wait with anticipation." Tracey looked at Ella quizzically "Well who are you playing with?" she asked. "Me, I'm partnering Tanya's husband, Mark Barcroft… he thinks he's got the best swing on the course, if not the best in Whittley Green! Ah! me! These boys have got a lot to learn." Ella addressed the ball and it sored towards the green, it landed a short putt away from the flag, she nodded with satisfaction and turned to Tracey "Your turn to tee off." Tracey placed the ball and tried to emulate Ella, the ball landing like Karen's near the edge of the green. "I wonder if Norma will play. She used to only play with Rodney." The ladies began to walk to the green as Tracey asked the question and Ella stopped in her tracks, "Oh poor Norma...I wonder who could partner her and bring her back to the club?"

The question was left unanswered as the course was covered, but it had to be addressed. Norma had become like a sacred icon to the Ladies Art and Cultural Society, they were not about to leave her out, Oh! No! They were on the contrary, diligently trying to keep her involved, participating and at the centre of things.

It was to this end that all the ladies gathered at Penguino's for a light lunch (any pasta or pizza for £4.99). Ella of course ordered an *ensulata* salad and *Perrier* water, as she toyed with the salad, she pondered out loud "Well, we need someone who won't mind loosing and who will treat Norma with kindness and understanding. That's not Jason, or Mark or Giles for that matter so who can we persuade to partner her ...any ideas?"

The group sat silently eating for a good minute or two, when Julia placed her tortellini fork down, she rubbed her chin and sighed before she made her suggestion. "I've been thinking about James a lot since Rodney's funeral. He's been rather attentive and considerate, in fact, I think it's made him realize that marriage is a partnership and that time together is precious. He's a bit like Rodney in that he's a man of few words and he often finds it difficult to express his feelings,...If you like I'll ask him, as a favour to me to take Norma as his doubles partner. Don't tell Norma until it's arranged though as I'm sure James would like to do that himself."

Tanya looked questioningly at Julia, one eyebrow raised. "You mean to say the errant golfer has altered?. Well I can't say that for Mark, he's still the little boy who wants to play boys games and to be the best at everything he plays. He maybe 54 years old but he's going on 8, I'm his mother substitute really, not his wife, and certainly not his lover!"

Karen McNaulty seemed really pleased with the idea of James Halifax partnering Norma, it would, she said pull all the threads together, and make the challenge of the ladies mixed doubles most interesting; she couldn't wait to get Jason Doupe on the green and to watch his balls fly!

Julia put the proposition of partnering Norma in the mixed doubles to James, and as she asked him she noticed for the first time, how old he was looking and how world weary he seemed. He sat quietly drumming his fingers on the edge of his laptop, he pursed his lips together and then smiled, "why not, she's a quiet, safe player, we'll get round the course and enjoy the scenery, and the lady deserves to be taken under our wing…you've looked after her well since Rodney's funeral." There was a long pause while James drummed his fingers, he was looking at Julia almost sadly as he continued "I know we don't say much about it love, but this growing old ain't easy, and I do still feel the same way about you as I felt thirty years ago… it's just that I don't know how to show it!"

Julia felt a surge of tenderness overwhelm her, her eyes filled with tears and spilt over onto James's balding head as she gently hugged him. "Don't ever leave me Julia… I know I'm a boring old fart and I don't appreciate the things you do or like, but I'll try I promise!" Julia realized James would do anything to keep her, even perhaps give up golf! She laughed as she teasingly said "Well I'll not make you give up golf! Just try to keep it to two games a week…I've got my interests and you have yours, it keeps us young and on our toes... Will you phone Norma and arrange to partner her? You can tell her I'll even come and watch!" James gave Julia an affectionate squeeze of the hand and a slight smile, it was enough, they were in this together and in touch with each other again, Norma had brought them together again.

Chapter Eighteen.

Carlo Tells His Story and Introduces Giovanni.

Norma sat in the armchair Rodney had died in; she was sipping a small glass of Barolo and nibbling a few small cubes of Blacksticks. Mr Poncepé sat by her side eating some strong Lancashire crumbly on crispy bread (he was making rather a mess) he sipped a little *Barolo* too.

The two old pals were deep in thought; they had much to think about. Carlo had bought the run down electric shop next to the cheese shop and had already gained a licence to sell wine. He would, he told Norma, open in six weeks' time. The Italian wine shop next to the Lancashire cheese shop, the enterprise would fulfil all Norma's ideas and give Toni an income for life. Norma so gentle, placid and unassuming was beside herself with joy, "oh! Mr Poncepé oh! I don't know what to say! Oh! My Rodney would be so bowled over!" She sighed and giggled again and again, clasping her hands together and then dabbing the tears from her eyes with a large man's hanky, she said "you're an angel, that's what you are, a kind old guardian angel...we can't pay you back yet but we will... I promise we will!"

"Stop it! Stop it! Norma please! I've something I have to tell you... you don't know much about me and my business, so let me tell you my story!" Carlo looked at Norma and wiped away the tears that slipped quietly down to his large moustache; he took a deep breath and sighed a long sad sigh.

"You know I'm a bald, fat, old man Norma...I'm seventy one years old...but I wasn't always fat and old. In Venice in 1960 I was a young handsome bull... a stylish clever wine waiter in a fashionable tourist part of the city. I was very handsome, very arrogant and very reserved. I didn't speak much English then, and I thought the tourists were brash, and very vulgar, especially the English. They were easy to make love to, so the other waiters said, anyway I didn't want that, I wanted a real woman a Sophia Loren type woman.

That July my whole life changed, for there at table *numero uno* was a party of English girls; eight of them, all in their early twenties. Norma, they were so loud and so common, with their high hairstyles and low cut dresses and so much make up, the Italian families were all 'tutting' and crossing themselves; it's funny now remembering, but, at the end of the table sat this gorgeous big titian blonde…she was so beautiful her bright eyes sparkling …and she smiled at me and shook her head. I came over and poured her some very strong Chianti. The girls wailed "How can you drink that stuff! Give us some *Asti*! Or *Lambrusco*, none of that Italian crap!" She looked at me and shook her head and said "Sorry" in Italian, they're stupid take no notice.

I was captured then, spell bound by her smile. I took her on my moped to a vine yard in the hills, and we tasted good wine, good food sitting in the long grass enjoying the real Italy. She said she was a buyer for a grocery business in Clitheroe, and that she was going to introduce some Italian wines, good wines. Tasty wines, she leaned over and kissed me… I kissed her on the lips back, and she laughed, she said "I can taste the good wine of Italy on your tongue Carlo", and she seduced me in the long grass. I gained my manhood and lost my heart right there. I would follow her to the ends of the Earth, and I did…to Clitheroe!

We lived and worked hard setting up our own wine cellar. She was wonderful my Georgina, a big bonny Lancashire lass who worked and loved with gusto. We married in 1965, and we were happy so happy, Norma, just one sad disappointment, we try and try but no baby comes. We go to doctors and hospitals and they say there is nothing wrong, Georgina should lose a little weight, that's all. So we get on with life, thinking we will not be blessed. We make lots of money and we build a good business, and then in 1981 I am forty one and my Georgina is forty five, we are told she is not ill, she is pregnant! Oh! God! Our joy our ecstasy.

Georgina was so happy, blossoming, blooming, and beautiful. When she went into labour I stayed with her for a long time, but they marched me out in the evening, she was so tired. I waited and waited and in the early hours of the morning they came to me with my son. He was big, beautiful and pink. And my Georgina, she was dead, a massive heart attack they said, she never saw her son.

Mr Poncepé had tears silently rolling down his cheeks as he told his story, and Norma was stroking his hand and wiping away her own tears and saying Oh! And sighing every so often.

"Giovanni Poncepé is a big blond man now, but when he was only a few days old the doctors say that his birth was too long and difficult, they say he will not develop well and he will not see. I sit by my Georgina's grave and I tell her I'm so sorry that bringing this child into the world has cost her life, and for what! For him to be a vegetable? No! I will work and work for our son! He will be right! He will be big and strong! And you know what Norma I keep my word. He's not a vegetable, he's clever, he's nearly thirty now and I'm so proud of him". Carlo stood up and paced a few steps back and forth, he turned and looked at Norma and took another deep breath saying "It's just that he's very shy, very timid and he's blind!... I try to be a good father to my Giovanni, but he needs young people and I'm old Norma, and he's lonely! So I want the wine cellar to be his as well as Toni's."

There was a long pause and a silence that was only broken by Carlo's sobs. Norma took Carlos hand and squeezed it; she gave him a hug and said "Eh! Come on love! Bring him home, he needs to meet the family!"

On the following Friday Carlo arrived at the lovely old stone cottage, Norma was in the garden overlooking Bestwood

91

and the rugged hills that surrounded it. She turned and smiled a welcome to Carlo, her arms held out in welcome "Come on in love!" She passed Carlo by as she spoke. And hugged the shy giant by his side, Giovanni smiled, his beautiful face lit up. He couldn't see Norma, but he could certainly feel her warmth and gentleness. He was, for the first time in his short life, held to the breast of a loving woman. Carlo Poncepé looked on in benign happiness.

Just at that moment the phone rang, it was James Halifax inviting Norma to be his partner in the ladies mixed doubles competition. Norma felt pleased that someone would partner her, and because it was Julia's husband, she felt confident enough to say yes, after all James had been really so very kind to her at the funeral.

Norma explained to Giovanni her dilemma, she had only taken up golf to please Rodney, and to get him out and about at least once a week. Now there was no need to attend the golf club really; except for Tracey, Ella, Karen, Tanya and Julia. They'd all been so kind and supportive. She really couldn't let them down, so she'd play in the competition and attend the captains day dinner, on one condition, that Mr Poncepé and Giovanni would be her guests. Giovanni was about to shyly refuse her offer, when the door was knocked or rather softly kicked.

It was Toni Borghini returning from Penguino's she was holding a large tray of lasagne. She had made it especially for Norma and Carlo; she beamed at Carlo and Norma and placed the tray on the laid table. She said in broken English "it needs some fifteen minutes in the hot oven to warm", it was as she turned to say this she caught sight of Giovanni , who rose out of his chair and bowed to her.Tonis head immediately went down, her hair falling over the scared and pitted skin of her cheeks and chin. She was unaware that he couldn't see her face, and that he was as painfully shy and awkward as she was around people. "I go in the kitchen and

92

prepare the salad as well." Norma and Carlo could see she was flustered and Norma was about to follow into the kitchen when Carlo went through first.

He spoke to Toni in Italian, fast and low, telling her he wanted her to meet his son. He took her hand and whispered pleadingly in her ear very quietly "please, Toni my son is blind and painfully shy I must bring him with me, don't turn away from him he needs to know young people!"

He brought Toni into the cosy living room and pulled her over to Giovanni. He introduced her in Italian to Giovanni and gave him her hand. Giovanni was overcome with embarrassment, his face was hot and flushed, and he stammered and blushed, pushing his blonde curly locks off his forehead. It was obvious he didn't know how to behave in front of women. Toni knew there was nothing to be afraid of here, she held Giovanni's hand and said in her husky Italian voice "I didn't know Carlo had a son, let alone such a big handsome one, come sit by me and tell me how you like my pasta."

Carlo and Norma were thrilled and desperate for Toni not to upset, or be upset by forming this friendship. Carlo poured out some Barolo for everyone even Toni, he raised his glass and said "I give you a toast to the Italian wine cellar and the Lancashire cheese shop, a joint venture for all of us." He noticed how Toni put the wine goblet into Giovanni's hand and how she smiled at him and how Giovanni seemed relaxed and sipped his wine and looked at Toni with unseeing eyes. He in turn whispered to Norma "I think it's going to work."

Toni sat with Giovanni and placed the Lasagne on his plate, she talked to him quietly in Italian; it seemed so easy for her, she told him whereabouts the food was on his plate and he lost his initial embarrassment as she teasingly spoon fed him the first portion of her pasta. "Well what do you think to my pasta?" she asked, and Giovanni grinned "It's made by an angel! Because it's the best I've ever tasted, Papa can't make pasta like this!"

"It's O.K. I teach you… tomorrow you come with me to Penguino's kitchen and I show you how to make pasta." Toni was a different woman with Giovanni; freed from the dread of being seen as ugly and repulsive, and knowing that this gentle giant was even more awkward around people than she was, gave her the chance to forget her own predicament, she felt secure and confident. And Giovanni, well he had never been so happy.

Chapter Nineteen.

Pasta is Blended and a Relationship Formed.

Toni collected Giovanni from the wine cellar in Clitheroe. Carlo and Giovanni both seemed like excited little boys. Carlo, because he saw his son making the effort to meet people and enjoy a woman's company, and Giovanni because this woman was treating him like a man and not a blind imbecile. He held her hand as a young man, not an invalid, and she took him to the little mini laughing, "You know it's a clapped out mini, Gio… you'll have a job squeezing in it! "She playfully pushed him into the front seat and he felt her strong hands easing him in the seat. Her hair fell on his face and it smelt of Jasmine and cocoanut, and all this was a wonderful new experience for him, he was blissfully happy.

Toni waved to Carlo and drove off to Penguino's; where Antonio Ullivari had told his staff to let Toni guide Giovanni, they were to talk to him and help him in the lay out of the kitchen, but they were to leave Toni and Gio to learn to work together. The waiters stifled a nudge, nudge, wink, wink expression, and Antonio warned he wouldn't have it! He knew that this relationship was equally important for Toni as for Gio, it would he hoped redress the balance a little, she would see that some men were gentle and innocent.

Antonio Ullivari had known Carlo Poncepé for many years as his vintner, but he had not known about Carlo's son until recently and now he hoped that he and his waiters could help Giovanni become a little more independent and more able to socialize with younger people. He asked his staff to be extra kind and gentle with Carlo's son and to give any advice and help where possible, but to let Toni be his mentor and guide.

When Toni and Gio arrived in the little mini the whole crew of waiters were lined up by the bar of Penguino's. They cheered as the couple entered, and Giovanni immediately

95

blushed and bowed his head. Toni became her harsh gruff old self in the kitchen… she said in her husky guttural Italian "O.K. you lazy, good for nothing, Italian louts why aren't you working? I've told Giovanni that you're all fast and the best waiters in Lancashire...so prove it!"

The waiters came forward and shook Giovanni by the hand; he in turn smiled in shy relief.

Antonio Ullivari suggested that Vincenco take him to the store room and kit Giovanni out in the chefs' trousers jacket and bandana. The four waiters disappeared with Giovanni and Toni shouted after them "he's big so make sure he has the right size!"

Fifteen minutes and a lot of laughing and joking later Giovanni reappeared, looking actually quite dishy in harlequin pants, a very large white t-shirt, a little black cap and white mules. Toni asked why was every one laughing and Gio lifted his t-shirt to show how the pants had a very wide gap at the front that exposed his Y fronts.

"I think we must take Giovanni into the town and get him properly kitted out! But for now that will have to do… Welcome to the kitchen Gio …Toni will show you what to do! Ok work every one." Antonio Ullivari clapped his hands and suddenly the restaurant was a hive of activity, preparing the dining room for the lunch hours and most of all preparing the food for the menu.

Toni led Gio round the kitchen letting him feel along the wide work surfaces, she counted the steps they took, out loud so when they had reached ten steps they came to the first range of hobs. Giovanni said "I know I can feel the heat as we approach." She guided him round the kitchen and explained all the implements, and then Toni asked Gio to try and walk round on his own and to say where he was. It was nerve racking to watch, but Toni let Gio go; amazingly he walked round saying where each item of equipment was.

96

"Ok! Gio now we go to the marble work surface and we make pasta together, you must listen and feel! I teach you I am your eyes and you are my hands ok."They stood by the marble surface and Toni held Giovanni's hand open, she poured a little of the fine flour into his hands telling him to feel the soft fine silkiness of it, "The flour must be soft, pure, very fine no grittiness or lumps, so now we make a mountain on the work top, make a hole a well in it, like so!" again she guided Gio's large hands to the flour letting him feel the mound and letting him make the well. "Now Gio we take the eggs and crack them into the well, be careful no shells ok!" Toni handed Giovanni an egg, he cracked it open and released the yolk into the well, followed by the other five very quickly. Toni marvelled at the way he managed, with unseeing eyes, to ensure the eggs broke cleanly and landed so neatly into the well.

"We come to the really clever bit now! We must mix and knead the dough, here I show you." Toni stood behind Giovanni, as she had behind Tracey, she slid her hands through his arms and began to mix and knead the dough all the time talking quietly in Gio's ear. Taking his hands; guiding and encouraging him to knead as well. Gio was enjoying this, he felt quite relaxed and at ease at first; but then as Toni whispered encouragement she pressed up against his back. He could feel the warmth of her body against him and the rhythmic movement of her arms, shoulders and torso caused a strange sensation in his own body that he had never felt before. Giovanni became embarrassed even a little agitated he was flustered and tried to stop the rhythmic kneading, panting "is it not ready yet?" Toni absorbed in the process hadn't realised the impact she had made on Gio. She pecked his cheek and called to all the staff to come see Gio's pasta mix … The waiters cheered and clapped, but they noticed that it wasn't just the pasta mix that had risen. They patted him on the back and told him he was a natural. Giovanni hot and blushing asked if he could try to make another batch on his own. Toni misreading his embarrassment didn't realize the problem she had created. "O.K. Gio I stand near you and watch, we make beautiful pasta aye! You and me, we work well together eh!"

Poor Gio; his face was now quite crimson and little beads of sweat were appearing at his temples; why did he feel so excited? Why was his body tingling so? And Toni unknowingly added to his ecstasy, by cupping his face and cheeks in her floured hands, gave him an encouraging kiss!

It was just about getting too much for Gio, when Antonio Ullivari came into the kitchen. He saw Gio's predicament immediately, he told Toni to give Gio a five minute break as he wanted to have a quick word with him to discuss uniforms etc.

He took Giovanni into his small snug office, and guided him to an easy chair, and poured him a coffee. Gio was still confused about his feelings, but he gratefully took the strong coffee Antonio handed him.

"I know it's difficult for you Gio, but you're doing fine, don't worry or panic Gio, because everything is new to you, you'll learn and get used to everything. I promised your father we'd look after you and Toni has promised that too Gio. She's a kind lovely woman Gio…"Antonio took a long gulp of coffee and pondered over how to tell Gio a little more about Toni. "Life has been cruel to Toni, Gio…men in particular have been bestial…her father he threw boiling pasta water at her in a drunken rage, it went all over her face…she's very badly scarred, and so she thinks she's ugly now and hides her face…but it's not just her face Gio that was hurt, it was her self-esteem. Recently she has suffered even more abuse, terrible abuse…I can't tell you, maybe Carlo can tell you! But Gio please stay look after Toni, encourage her to be a woman and not a gruff hard chef; we can see she wants to help you, and befriend you.. So let her, and enjoy! Talk to Carlo, he'll be pleased with what you've achieved today."

Giovanni was grateful for Antonio's brief explanations and encouragement, he was still confused and concerned about these new sensations that he was feeling and was with trepidation going to speak with his father to ask what and how he should overcome these strange strong emotions he felt. Yes! He would speak to Carlo this evening; meantime he would try to master his pasta making and his bodies growing awareness and desire for Toni and her rhythmic kneading body movements.

Antonio Ullivari took Toni to one side and told her very gently "Go steady Toni- the boy isn't used to people or to the hustle and bustle of our kitchen, give him time. You've been able to get him to leave his father's side and to face the kitchen, well done, just keep encouraging and supporting him, but we don't want to overwhelm him. So tomorrow you take him with Vincento to town and kit him out O.K.! And maybe ask Carlo if you can get him some new underwear and clothes that make him look like a trendy Italian and not a middle aged misfit-No! Perhaps I'd better ask Carlo that!" Toni smiled and shrugged her shoulders "O.K! I'll get him to make some batches of dough for tomorrow and I'll see if Carlo will let us loose on the town!"

Gio breathed deep and asked Toni if he could try to make the next batch of pasta mix on his own, she could tell him if he was going wrong, meantime she could be making tortellini and ravioli. "And so Giovanni's first day in the kitchen moved on, with Gio beginning to fit into this Italian hurly-burly whirlwind atmosphere of Penguino's kitchen, furthermore he was beginning to enjoy it. He felt comfortable with Toni's gentle encouragement, even though her voice was like liquid gravel, her words were gentle tender and supportive. He wanted to be close to her, but he found it difficult to control these strange feelings and Stirrings that passed over him in waves.

The waiters and chefs stood nearby watching and giggling at Gio's flustering embarrassment, but Antonio quietly warned them he'd fine anyone who dared to say a word to Gio or Toni about the relationship, "Leave them alone! And let nature take its course" was Antonio's final order and Penguino's staff happily obeyed.

At 7.30 Toni asked Antonio if she could take Giovanni to Carlo. She had prepared all the sources and pastas, and marinated the various cuts of meat and fish, the chefs knew what to do, and she would be back in an hour. Toni so wanted to tell Carlo and Norma just how well Gio had performed in the kitchen (she hadn't realized just how well) and to ask if he could be taken for his uniform and new clothes. Antonio saw how jubilant and happy Toni was, he hoped and prayed that this was going to be a budding relationship, maybe God willing, a budding romance.

He waved the happy pair off, telling Gio to ask his father if Toni and Vincenco could take him shopping. As the little mini disappeared Antonio went into the office and rang Carlo's mobile. He gave Carlo a little potted version of what had transpired during the day and asked if he, Carlo might tell Gio of Toni's misfortune, he would leave it up to Carlo.

When the little mini pulled up outside the Lancashire cheese shop Carlo was there waiting for them and Norma. They both stood by the door an air of excitement and a look of questioning anticipation on their faces.

Toni got out the mini first and dashed round to Gios side, she helped him out excitedly, saying, almost shouting to Carlo "He's great Carlo… he's a natural pasta maker, all the waiters say so! We're great together, we're a team!"(All this was said in very fast Italian) Giovanni was smiling with embarrassment, how was he going to explain his feelings, and ask how to control them, and what should he do about them?

Carlo translated Toni's excited Italian statements to Norma, who gave Giovanni a motherly hug and Toni one as well. "Mr Ullivari, Antonio, says can you hurry back Toni, they're very busy- Oh! Yes and you can take Giovanni to get kitted up, so you don't need to go in to the kitchen till three o'clock tomorrow!"

Toni felt and looked disappointed, she wanted to tell Carlo how well Gio had done, but she realized that Antonio had already done that, and got permission for the shopping expedition tomorrow. "Oh! O.K., I just want you to know how well we got on... making pasta, we make a great team, don't we Gio?" She squeezed Giovanni from behind and gave him an affectionate peck on the cheek. "I'll come round for you at 9 o'clock tomorrow, O.K. Gio! You be ready waiting! Chow!" With that Toni went back to the mini and drove quickly off, leaving a blushing and stammering Gio to ask Carlo and Norma what he was to do about these strange emotions that were stirring in his mind and body (especially his body!)

Chapter Twenty.

Giovanni's emotions are Described and Carlo and Norma Explain.

Carlo put an affectionate arm around his sons shoulder. He was so proud and pleased that Gio had taken the first steps to overcome his fears and timidness. He could see that Giovanni had made great inroads towards his independence and towards entering a wider social life… all new, unknown and exciting for him. Carlo asked questioningly in Italian "Well Gio! How was your first day of freedom; Away from your tired old Papa?"

Gio turned to face his beloved father; he wanted to tell him so much and to ask him so much as well, he began by stammering and mumbling in Italian.

"I like Toni very much and Antonio and all the staff… I have a good day, it's all so noisy, fast, and hot, everyone is busy, busy… I don't know if I'm in the way, perhaps I'm not good being there? Antonio he called me in his office to tell me I'm O.K. and he says I must talk to you… about Toni, you will tell me about her? Papa I like Toni, but when she stands near me and touches me… Oh! Papa I feel strange, not in control of myself, I am shaking and sweating, things are happening to me!"

Norma was watching Giovanni very closely especially when she heard Toni's name, she couldn't understand what was said but she could tell Gio was struggling and embarrassed. Norma being Norma and full of northern curiosity and motherliness just asked Carlo to explain what had been said in English. "Don't be shy lad just say what's to do, and we'll help you!" Norma said directly to Giovanni. Carlo then had to retell Gio's feelings and Antonio's request about telling Gio of Toni's resent ordeal. Carlo led Gio into the cheese shop and got the chairs out. Carlo was struggling to start to explain to Gio what had happened to Toni, when gentle kind old Norma took over. She held Gio's hand and pulled him to one of the chairs saying "Hutch up lad and listen, Carlo and I are going to tell you everything about Toni… But before we start I want a promise from you, that you won't hurt or upset my girl, that you'll still be friends with her, kind and understanding, right …have I got that promise?"

Gio didn't know what was about to be unfolded before him, but he did know he liked Toni and he didn't want to lose her friendship only so freshly made. So he stammered his promise to Norma telling her he wanted to keep Toni's friendship more than ever.

Norma told Giovanni all about Toni's father and how he had beaten and abused her and her mother. Toni had seen her mother sexually abused and tormented by her own father, and because of this, she hated men. She had learnt to live with this abhorrence of men by becoming almost masculine in her own behaviour and dress; coupled with her facial disfigurement and scaring and her physical stature, she'd become one of the boys at Penguinos. It was the only way she could cope with her life! When Antonio introduced her to the Ladies Italian Society she had appeared so strong, self-assured and in control. She had befriended Tracey especially when she had found out that Tracey was suffering the same kind of abuse as she had suffered from her husband. Norma didn't go into details of Toni and Tracey's friendship, only to say that Toni had gone to live with Tracey to protect her.

Norma and Mr Poncepé looked at each other and both took a deep breath, Norma continued in a strangled voice "It was after my Rodney's funeral…we were all upset, Tracey was holding my arm and crying and Toni just wiped away the tears and kissed her on the cheek, when Jason Doupe took Tracey away! We didn't know that he was ragging mad! Well he… he did terrible terrible things to Tracey….. And when

103

Toni went to the house to rescue her, he did the same to her only worse!" Norma was sobbing uncontrollably now and Carlo put his arms round her saying "its O.K. Norma...I'll finish for you... I tell him in Italian...I promise O.K."

Giovanni didn't need to hear more really, he had already decided he would stick by Toni; he would suppress his desires and learn to control these strange emotions. He huskily said to Norma "I stick by Toni! I promise I'll look after her as she looks after me!" Sweet, soft, sentimental old Norma put her arms round Giovanni and hugged him, till he was covered in her grateful tears. Carlo blew his nose hard.

"Come on" he said "Let's close the shop ... I take you home Norma, will you tell Toni Gio will be ready and waiting outside the Cellar with some money, she can turn him into a fine Italian handsome man!" Carlo closed the shop, took Norma home and then drove to Clitheroe.

On the way he told Giovanni some of the awful things that had happened to Toni, how she'd lost her virginity, her pride, her dignity and all her self-esteem. Jason Doupe had used her like an animal. Toni was now at the very lowest point and if he, Gio turned away from her, Carlo worried that she might do something drastic.

Gio listened, his sightless eyes closed, but he rocked backwards and forwards in anguish, he realized that Toni had been very brave when she took him to Penguinos... she was strong wonderfully so ... he liked her even more. He had to tell Carlo about the very strong emotions and effects she was having on him, both mental and physical.

"Papa I want to stay with Toni at Penguinos, and to learn more and to be part of everything... it's good I enjoy it... but I don't know, it's all so new, and I'm not in control! ...of myself!... especially when Toni does things to me!" Gio almost whispered the last part of what he was saying. Carlo pressed the brake pedal gently; he needed to slow down to listen more attentively. "O.K. Gio, try to tell me what Toni is doing that makes you feel out of control?"

Poor Gio, he struggled, stammered and squirmed as he described how Toni had shown him how to knead the dough, he stammered even more when Carlo asked him how this had affected him, but he managed to explain the strange effects it was having on his body. Carlo was by now unable to stifle and suppress his amusement, as Gio described his body's reactions; in fact, he had to stop the car. He began to laugh as he said "It's O.K. Gio …that's wonderful, you are a man and these reactions are normal, perfectly normal, especially as you like her. Just enjoy her company and be kind to her, and respect her, remember she is scared of men, she is as scared of you as you are of her, and she's been very badly mauled. I tell you more about that in a few more weeks, just now, get to know her and enjoy each other's company, yes!"

Carlo felt it wasn't right to tell Gio that Toni was pregnant, not yet. Gio was still an innocent boy in a man's body, entering into an adult world that viewed sexual gratification as an everyday occurrence. Carlo's perception of these activities was to consider them as outrageous, provocative but above all so demeaning to men and women. He worried that Gio being blind missed much of these things, and now was having to understand and come to terms with this adult world. He hoped and prayed that Gio would not be seduced or ruined by this world, and that he would learn about love before desire; Carlo fervently hoped too that Toni would be Gio's guide and mentor.

Chapter Twenty one.

Toni Turns a Blind Boy Into a Prince
& Gio Makes a Conquest.

Toni arrived at Carlos wine cellar with Vincenzo the head waiter in the back of the little mini. She got out of the car and eagerly took Gio's hand, she laughingly asked "Have you got plenty money Gio? 'cause I'm going to turn you into the best dressed man in Lancashire!"

She slid her arm through his and playfully coaxed him into the front seat. Gio was happy, he trusted Toni's judgement and guidance, (he had to he couldn't see) he was relying on her. Vincenzo was the head waiter at Penguinos, a small, friendly and cheerful Italian who resembled Charlie Chaplin. He joked with Gio all the way to Preston, telling him he'd make sure he looked trendy! But not like a puff you know! Toni defended Gio, saying "this man is so handsome…you couldn't make him look bent if you tried! Don't worry Gio; I will make sure you're the best dressed Italian in town."

The little mini was parked near to Avenham Park, and the Italian trio walked amiably through Winkley Square in the bright morning sunshine of a bright and beautiful summer day.

Toni held Gio's hand and swung his arm happily, they seemed like any young couple enjoying their free time in the sun, and Toni, well she was enjoying every moment (it was as if a magic veil had waved over her, and she was able to forget her scars, Gio couldn't see her, he liked her for herself, and he trusted her!)

They visited the main catering store in Preston, and had Giovanni kitted out in a very snazzy chef's outfit that fitted perfectly. Vincenzo helped Gio try it on and jokingly said "No exposed 'Y' fronts this time! aye! Gio! That's the next thing; let's get to M&S for essential undies!"   Toni and Gio walked side by side into the large store, Toni guiding him on and up the escalator. Gio was a little scared he'd never been on one before, but Toni whispered "It's O.K. Gio I'll tell you when to step off!" She was his eyes, and his trust in her was absolute, like a child's unquestioning trust of a mother. They let Vincenzo shop for the undies and socks, a dozen pairs in packs of 3. Toni called Vincenzo over to them, and told him that they were going to wander up and down Friargate looking at all the men's shops to see what was best, and then they'd go in and choose what suited Gio the best. Vincenzo didn't want to be a wallflower and said "I'll leave you two to get on with it then, make sure you don't make him look gay!...see you later at Penguinos."

Gio held Toni's hand and pulled her closer to him. "I'm glad he's gone, he's a nice guy, but he's always joking! And I don't know if he's just making fun of me or not!...I trust you Toni... you won't make me look stupid!" Toni came even closer to Gio and looked into his trusting blind face, she softly said "I'm looking after you, Carlo and Norma have entrusted you to me and they're going to be so proud of you.... Almost as proud as me! Come on Gio let's turn you into my prince!"

Five shops later, and £400 lighter, Gio and Toni walked back towards Winkley Square. They were flushed with happiness, Gio dressed in the best of his purchases, slate grey designer jeans, and an Armani top and Nike trainers. An Armani jumper casually draped over his shoulders, three shopping bags in one hand, and his other arm through Toni's. He looked and felt the best man about town.

Toni had bought some sandwiches and coffee from Alex's little delicatessen take away bar. They found a low wooden bench at the top of the square, and sat bathed in the warm summer sunlight. Toni sat tightly pressed against Gio; she smiled at him and leaned over to his face with a *pannettone* chicken sandwich in her hand. "Do you want the chicken and salad or the cheese and salami? Or shall we just share a bit of both?" she asked. Gio turned towards her voice, and as he did so his face brushed into her beautiful auburn hair, and he laughed as he rubbed his face in it. "Oh, Toni! I love the smell of your soft soft hair...You know it's at times like this, that I really wish, I really long to be able to see! I feel the warmth. I feel the sun...I feel your hair...I feel the gentleness of your hands and your arms, and I long to see. I hear the happiness in your voice and the kindness as you talk to me... and Oh God! I want so much for you to like me...I have to trust you, but I would love to see you!"

Toni's hand was held in Gio's, she was overwhelmed by what he had just said, touched by his tenderness and his obvious longing for her. She was painfully aware of her own physical appearance; she knew she was ugly, disfigured and unsightly. She sighed as the tears fell from her eyes. "Oh Gio! I don't think you'd feel the same about me, if you could see... I'm not a pretty sight!" Gio reached up to her hair and ran his fingers through it, he raised it to his face and smelt it and then he brought it to his lips and kissed it. "I will never know what colour is! But I feel you hair and it makes my throat tight, because it's part of you! It makes my heart leap!" He let his hand fall and as it fell Gio touched Toni's cheek, and his fingers, so sensitive to touch, felt the warmth of her skin and the wetness of her tears. He gently caressed her forehead and cheek with the tips of his fingers, "Oh! Toni I feel the soft warmth of your cheeks, they are beautiful to me, they are warm and tender and I love them, because they are you!" This was said in a choked whisper. He took her hand and kissed it, "Please Toni can I be part of you, can you be my eyes?" Toni tried not to be soft, she tried to be the gruff chef, but as she looked into Gio's unseeing eyes she knew she'd do anything and everything for this gentle blind giant. "O.K. Gio I'm yours!" Toni laughed through her tears and kissing him on the cheek said "we're a team; we're going to do everything together!"

They ate their sandwiches in a pleasing silence, each feeling the glowing warmth of friendship. Gio now understood his father's advice to be kind and respectful of Toni. He was looking forward to life with Toni. Toni was feeling content, she felt at ease with this man who cared for her so much, and she knew that he depended on her to enter into the seeing world.

They went arming along the winding pathway that passed through the square, the warm early afternoon sun gently toasting their upturned faces. Toni rang Carlo telling him they were returning to Penguinos to prepare for the evening menus. She laughed happily when Carlo asked had Gio got a chefs uniform, she handed the mobile to Gio, who informed him it was a master chefs outfit (it was the only one big enough to fit him) and Toni added "He looks gorgeous! Quite a dish himself!"

Antonio Ullivari met them at the entrance to Penguinos, "I'm glad your back, we've a party of eight business men here (some of them are from Milan) and they're wanting some good pasta dishes! So you two into the kitchen quick and make the best pasta dishes out side of Italy!" So Toni's dream of parading Gio in his new finery was thwarted, it would have to wait till later at Norma's. Gio quickly changed (with Vincenzo's help) into his new chefs outfit, he looked the part; he went swiftly and easily to the marble topped work bench, where Toni had already placed the eggs and flour out for him. Antonio watched in wonder, as Gio and Toni worked in unison to produce beautiful light textured pasta, delicate yet tasty, they began rolling and shaping the pasta. They were completely absorbed in their work.

The happy pair were so busy they didn't notice Carlo and Norma entering the restaurant, and they didn't see the sheer joy and pride expressed on Carlo's face; but they did hear Norma's ecstatic exclamation of pleasure at Gio's conversion to a master pasta chef. Norma and Carlo were like eager little children waiting to see Santa, they were desperate to see how Gio and Toni had managed their first shopping expedition, and of course to see how their work at Penguino's was turning out!

Toni and Gio made quite a few pasta dishes, tasty spaghetti and succulent with a variety of sauces and ingredients, but one they made was especially for Norma and Carlo, *Spaghetti Gamberetti con Calamari*. The spaghetti pasta was light and tender with the taste of eggs and seasoning, but it was the sauce that the two chefs created, a delicious combination of crushed garlic, finally diced red onion, bay leaf, rosemary and good juicy plump fresh tomatoes, olive oil and a dash of strong red wine. Toni made it and most importantly, Gio tasted it, his judgement was given, and a few pinches of chilli added, it was stirred again, Gio tasted once more, he gave a smile of satisfaction kissing his finger tips to Toni. The *Gamberetti* and *Calamari* and baby squid added… it was heaven from the sea.

Toni served it up in a very large terrine and she and Gio carried it out together to the waiting table. Carlo and Norma were absolutely in heaven, the pride Carlo felt and audibly expressed. "My God! It's the pasta made in heaven, so light and so tasty! Did you make this Gio?"

Toni grinned and put her arm round Gio's shoulder "We made it! We make everything together! We're a perfect team!" As Toni said this Norma was placing a large forkful of spaghetti de mare into her mouth, she closed her eyes and tasted with her tongue and lips. "Oh! Toni! That even beats Barolo and Blacksticks combined! You're both wonderful!"

The Italian business men couldn't resist asking for the delicacy, the terrine was carried to their table and they served themselves with copious helpings. They applauded the chefs, calling them to their table. Toni and Gio bowed, both embarrassed by the attention and admiration. Antonio Ullivari came over and whispered to Gio "O.K. Gio you're hired, but you always work together!"

The business men left saying they would be bringing some of their most important clients with them next time to taste the true taste of Italy. They asked for the chefs names, Gio said (and loud enough for everyone to hear!) "We are Toni and Giovanni Poncepé the perfect pair of Master pasta chefs!" He turned to Toni and putting his strong arms round her he kissed her on the nose, because he couldn't see, he said "We're the best, a perfect team!"

Carlo and Norma raised their glasses (it was only mineral water not Barolo) and Carlo raising his voice in happiness said "to Toni and Gio the perfect team!" Norma just blew them a kiss and said to Carlo "well whose going to run the wine and cheese shop now?" Carlo smiled and raised Norma's hand to his lips he kissed her finger tips and said "Norma, you and I will struggle on I think we've a few more years yet ; besides I think I've sold the cellar in Clitheroe, it's too much work for an old man like me. Antonio has bought it with a mystery buyer!" Norma gasped with surprise, and then quietly thought for a few moments, she looked at Carlo searchingly and asked the question "Well who's going to buy the stock for the Italian wine cellar? And I hope they know where we get our Barolo!"

Carlo patted her hands and said "It's alright Norma I've got all the best connections we'll always have Barolo and Blacksticks. I think you and I are going to enjoy the wine and cheese shop in our old age! Maybe it's better that Gio and Toni have found what they love doing together; let them enjoy to and we'll always have good food and good wine." "Rodney and Georgina would like that!" Said Norma contentedly.

Chapter Twenty two.

Tracey takes charge of her future with the help of Ms McNaulty and Antonio Ullivari.

Tracey stood in the early morning sunshine and stared out towards the third flag. She breathed deeply, smiled broadly and addressed the ball. Her swing was smooth, sure and strong and the ball flew in a long arched drive that landed just off the green in the semi rough, on the edge of the fairway. "Oh well done Tracey! You're getting to be quite a match for Giles!" Ella was laughing as she said this. She and Karen McNaulty were delighted with Tracey's progress, both on and off the golf course. Ms' McNaulty noted with her analytical eye that Tracey's self-esteem and self-confidence were much in evidence these days. She was taking charge of her golf swing and her life, and it showed; no longer was she the shy, timid wall flower holding back any ideas or opinions, she was assertive and assured, the only obstacle obstructing her new life, was the fear she had, of her father's reaction to her impending separation with Jason.

"I'd happily divorce him, but I know that it would break my dad's heart! So I'll just accept a legal separation… and Jason can go to hell! Or as far away as possible."

Karen McNaulty smiled and shook her head, as she placed her driver in her golf bag; she started to walk down towards the green with Ella and Tracey. She had had numerous E- mails from Jason Doupe in the last week, all were leading to an out of court settlement; but the last e- mail had actually surprised Ms. McNaulty, in that Jason had asked for a mutually agreed divorce with an agreed financial settlement. Ms. McNaulty had told Tracey of this latest missive, and Tracey was now brooding over its implications and how it would affect her father. Karen McNaulty felt it was time she had a quiet informal chat with this old fashioned Irish business man, he couldn't be the fearsome father figure that Tracey seemed to think he was. Ms' McNaulty decided, as she searched for her ball, that a visit to Mr Murphy was really necessary. The ladies continued round the course until the ninth hole, when Ms McNaulty asked that they continue without her, as she had rather a pressing legal engagement, she would meet them on Friday at Penguinos for their usual entertaining Italian cultural evening.

Ella and Tracey continued their game of golf, and yes, Ella thought, Tracey really was very good, they made an excellent team, a formidable duo, something Whittley Green could be truly proud of.

Ms. McNaulty had telephoned Nick Murphy, explaining she was his daughter's friend and legal advisor, and could she have a little informal chat with him. Nick Murphy didn't know this lady or what the hell she was going to chat about? But if it concerned Tracey and she was in trouble, he needed to know and to help! So she'd better come to see him right now!

Two hours and three coffees later Nick Murphy was shaking Karen McNaultys hand, saying in a broad Irish accent "Get rid of the conniving little bastard, and don't give him any more than he deserves and that my dear if you'll excuse my French, is feck all! I'll go and see Trace and ask her to forgive me for believing the snivelling toad! I'll make it up to her, I will, I will!"

Ms McNaulty knew she could bring this sad marriage and all its sorry state of affairs to a quick and satisfactory conclusion, the only thing she regretted was the fact that Jason Doupe would not be playing in the ladies mixed doubles competition, she would have to be content with the satisfaction of screwing his balls in the divorce court and not on the golf course. Ah well! A small price to pay for golf widows revenge! And anyway Nick Murphy said he would consider it a great honour to play with Ms McNaulty, he'd never played with a lady before let alone a lady captain! He was surely moving up in the world.

Tracey and Ella finished their round of golf at Whittley Green and decided to visit Penguinos for lunch. It would be a light (very light for Ella) lunch with perhaps a mineral water or cappocino.Tracey would return Ella home and then take an oral English class with fifteen Italian and Urdu speaking male teenagers, Tracey could face anything these days.

Antonio Ullivari held his arms out to the two ladies, he welcomed them in with hugs and kisses, lifting them off their feet and swirling them round. The party of Italian business men cheered and looked on in envious admiration, Antonio Ullivari was a true Italian. "Come on Antonio – introduce the ladies and let us share their company!" they called out. Antonio bowed to them, but said the ladies were here to meet Norma and Mr Poncepé, not to flirt with dangerous Italian gigolos. Ella lifted an eyebrow, smiled wickedly and said "Oh! I don't know Antonio; a little flirting with a few Italian Romeos might brighten my day!" She blew a kiss to them and walked sassily past them towards Norma, who was already laughing and pulling a chair up to the table.

Tracey was embraced with tender motherly concern "Well how are you? You're looking really well! Much better! So pretty!"

Norma was happy, she may not have had any children of her own but her maternal and caring nature was now being used to the full to care for her adopted family. Tracey was happy and contented with her old friend and new mother, she could talk to Norma about anything and everything, she wasn't judgemental, just full of empathy, and immensely practical. She listened as Tracey told her about the latest twist in her marriage. Tracey was able to express her concerns regarding her father's reactions to the break-up of the marriage. Norma just held her hand and patted her shoulder; she was just about to suggest she talk to her father when Nick Murphy himself walked into the restaurant.

Antonio Ullivari spoke quietly to the big Irish man, he nodded his head and led Mr Murphy through the dining area towards Tracey, and the two men were smiling as they came towards Norma's table.Traceys heart was pounding and she hid her face in her hands whispering "Oh! Please dad don't make a scene, don't be angry with me! Please!"

To her amazement, he put his arms round her, lifting her clean out of her chair, embracing her in a gentle bear hug saying "Oh! Trace Trace, why didn't you come to me years ago? Why didn't you tell me? You let me believe that snivelling lying bastard! Well don't you worry love, Karen's told me all, and I mean all, and she's shown me photos, so I know! I know what that swine did! You've endured hell from that man. I've told Mrs McNaulty to go ahead on your behalf and screw the bastard for as much as she can!" Tracey sobbed with relief, and Norma was patting the backs of both Tracey and Nick Murphy, Carlo sighed and poured out a glass of Barolo for himself and one for Nick, this was a lunch hour that had gone quite crazy! Would these golfing ladies ever be calm, rational and composed like Norma? He wondered.

Ella smiled sweetly and ate her Ceaser salad, she turned to Nick and said "You know Tracey's over the worst now; she's taken control of her situation and her golf! And I can tell you she's making a bloody fine job of both of them. Don't worry over Tracey Mr Murphy she's got good friends who'll see no harm comes to her."

"Well I know that!. . Mrs McNaulty, she's Tracey's solicitor …. She's explained everything, and she said she's going to enjoy screwing the balls off of that creep!... I just want to make sure she and my grandson aren't financially in trouble ….so Tracey, you need anything, you come to your

115

dad see and we'll sort it! But what I want to know is what about the other lass? What's going to happen to her? I want that swine to pay for that!"

Mr Poncepé was trying to explain how he had used the purchase of the wine cellar and the new found friendship of Norma, Tracey and Toni to introduce his clever but blind son to Toni, he hoped it would benefit his son and bring him into the wider world! Nick Murphy was rubbing his forehead in befuddled amusement and confusion, when Carlo grinned and held his hand out saying "see! Let my boy and Norma's girl explain, they tell you how things are working out! See they come to meet you!"

Toni and Gio came quietly over, Toni leading Gio by the hand; they smiled at Nick Murphy shyly but confidently safe in their new found partnership. Nick rose to greet them shaking both Toni's and Giros hand. "I want to know how I can help you. After what's happened to you I need to show my gratitude!" Toni shook her head vigorously and explained in broken English, that she and her Gio needed no financial help, they were a talented pair of chefs who would grace a master class on T.V, but Antonio Ullivari the restaurant owner had the good sense and the kindest heart to welcome them both into his restaurant, because he knew they were the best. "Would you like to try my Gio's latest creative pasta dish Mr Murphy?" Toni asked with obvious pride and Nick Murphy felt obliged to say "Yes of course!" even though the big man wasn't at all keen on pasta, he felt he had to show willing to this lady…after all she'd gone through hell to help his daughter.

The pair went back into the kitchen and soon returned with a large dish full of their latest creation.

Toni placed the dish in front of Nick saying "Enjoy", and then both she and Gio stood, watching and waiting for the big man to taste. Nick reluctantly raised a mouthful of the pasta delicacy to his lips; he shut his eyes ready to force himself to swallow the spoonful whole and not to taste, but too late, his taste buds aroused by the delectable juice enticed his tongue to feel the warm tingling inviting texture…ah me! He was a captured man. He opened his eyes wide, smiled broadly, like a cat that's found a pot of double cream, and proceeded to eat with gusto! Toni clapped with delight! She squeezed Gios hand, and he grinned, pleased that their culinary inspirational endeavours were appreciated by the big man himself.

It was at this moment that the Italian gentlemen party finally left and Ella blew them a farewell kiss. True to their romantic image they laughingly rushed over to her and each gave her a farewell hug and many kisses as they parted. "Well who were they?—they looked mighty important and very, very Italian! Did we impress them Antonio?" She quizzed him playfully, but Antonio grinned and touched the side of his nose and winked knowingly at Mr Poncepé. "A little venture has just started to be negotiated; I think a lot of prayers are going to be answered! But I might need to talk to you Nick I mean Mr Murphy in a few weeks' time."

Tracey looked at her watch and gasped "Oh! Christ! I've got to be in the centre of Preston in 15 minutes …will you settle up for me dad…. I'll see you later!"

Chapter Twenty three.

A Deal is Struck and a Secret Revealed.

A few weeks later Mr Poncepé, Antonio Ullivari, Ms McNaulty, Nick Murphy and Tracey sat round the marble table at Penguinos. It was 10.30 and the party were all given coffee and croissants. Everyone seemed to have some idea that a big change was about to happen, a change for the better, at least for Tracey, Toni and Gio.

Mr Poncepé sat next to Antonio Ullivari, the old man couldn't contain his excitement, he felt that all his worries regarding Gio were about to be solved, he was going to be able at long last, to relax and enjoy his life in retirement, he would take pleasure in his Italian wine cellar sipping Barolo with his good friend Norma and her Lancashire cheese shop.

Carlo knew his son was safe with Toni and that they would always have a home; Gio would have security, all he wanted now was to know that Toni would stay with his son, and he knew that that was Norma's wish as well; but he mustn't push them into anything, they seemed to be solving their own problems anyway

Nick Murphy sat between Tracey and Karen McNaulty. The big man was as happy as a pig in muck (as the big man himself said).He had been on the phone a good few hours these past few days, long and cordial discussions had passed with Antonio Ullivari, and they had arrived at quite a few deals; the upshot being Nick was to be the financial backer (on behalf of Tracey) for the purchase of Poncepé Wine merchants and Wine Importers of fine European Wines especially the *Barolo* region. Tracey would be the equal partner of this business with Antonio Ullivari, thus she would own her own legitimate business, one that would utilize her language expertise. And at the same time ensure that Toni would have shares in the enterprise. This enterprise would give

Tracey the independence she craved and the security Nick felt she required, Nick was a happy man!

Antonio Ullivari sat with Tracey as Ms McNaulty drew up the deeds and new contract that enabled the business venture to proceed. Ms McNaultys documents were in English, but Antonio needed an Italian translation for the Italian vineyard owners, they'd be arriving later, and would need copies to sign and exchange. He and Tracey sat with their laptop and translated the necessary articles and contracts. Antonio Ullivari smiled with pleasure and a growing sense of admiration began for Tracey Doupe, this young lady was not the shy simpleton of yesterday, but a pretty smart woman with an excellent command of Italian and what's more an even stronger command of the wine business. He would enjoy cementing their financial partnership, and he greatly enjoy talking business with her!

Toni and Gio were very busy in the hot and bustling kitchen, preparing pastas, sauces and pizza dough. They made various marinades for meat and fish dishes and they were beginning the preparation of the vegetables, this time was always heated and hectic. Toni felt hot and stressed, she was giving orders in her gruff Italian throaty voice, Gio was quietly kneading dough and folding it ready for cutting, he couldn't see Toni, but he felt her suddenly lean into him, he knew something was wrong! He felt her forehead, it was hot and clammy. She was gasping and sinking slowly down his arm to the floor. Gio shouted out for help in Italian, he held Toni in his arms and wished with all his heart that he could see... he needed to help his Toni!

All the kitchen staff crowded round Gio and Toni. It was Nick Murphy and Tracey who came in the kitchen and took control of the situation, the big Irish man just pushed through saying "move back! Move back and give the girl some air!" Tracey sat Toni up and wiped her brow with a damp cloth, and as Toni responded she gently said "Come on, love, let's take you to the rest room, we don't want you throwing up in your kitchen!" She raised Toni up and guided her to the rest room, and Toni sobbed in Italian "Oh! God I feel sick, I feel sick!"

Poor Gio, a look of panic, worry and shear bewilderment was written all over his face. Nick Murphy seeing his bewilderment patted him on the shoulder in a manly gesture and laughingly said "You'll have to get used to this lad! Tracey's mother was sick nearly every day when she was carrying Trace!"

Carlo Poncepé put his hands over his eyes and whispered a plea to the holy virgin; he didn't want Gio to find out like this! He really should have told him himself weeks ago! He came to Gio's side and took his sons hand, and Gio feeling the warmth of his father asked quietly "Is my Toni pregnant Papa?" But Carlo didn't answer and Gio continued "take me to her, I need to be with her now!" Carlo led him out of the kitchen saying "Don't be upset with Toni Gio it's not her fault, I should've told you, but you were so happy with her, I wanted you to be happy and stay with her, please forgive me!"

As Gio entered the rest room Toni had stopped retching and was breathing deeply as she sipped iced water. Tracey turned to Gio and took his hand and said, as she gave it to Toni. "We'll leave these two alone for a few minutes, she's O.K. Gio, just a bit faint, hold her to you for a while and then she'll be alright."Tracey led Carlo out before he could say anything "leave them alone Carlo, they'll be O.K. let them sort it out!"

Tracey started to close the door as Gio put his arms round Toni and pulled her to his big chest and kissed her lowered face. Tracey heard him say in Italian "You should have told me Toni, why didn't you tell me? "And she heard Toni's sobbing voice say "Because I didn't want to lose you, I didn't want you to leave me! And now you know you'll not want to be with me!"

They all sat round the table trying to listen and looked at the closed door. Carlo was anxiously rubbing his forehead. All that they had been doing to help his son was, he feared, now going wrong, he must speak to Gio and Toni, guide them to the right decision! He was just about to go back into the rest room when the door opened and Gio came out holding Toni's hand. "It's alright don't worry everyone, we're going to make lunch, we're fine the three of us!"

Carlo just flopped down onto his chair and wept with joy and relief, everything was going right! The deals were struck and the secret was out, he could at long last relax and stop worrying. As for Gio and Toni, he wondered what had been said, but they were obviously keeping that private, Gio would tell him later!

Chapter Twenty four.

The Mixed Doubles Competition,

The Golf Awards and the Captains Day Celebrations.

A sense of calm seemed to be restored and was passing over the Ladies Italian Cultural Appreciation Society. Two turbulent months had passed and its problems were now being resolved. Life was going back to normal, or in other words, golf seemed to be engulfing some of the ladies and their errant husbands once more!

Tanya found Marks' keen interest in Ella Smythe-Dawson and her handicap, amusing; she was deliciously anticipating how he would react to them on the golf course. She deliberately underplayed Ella's obvious talents, both the physical and the golf! Mark was becoming more and more obsessed with his own game, spending many hours (both on and off the golf course) practising his swing and stance. He watched endless D.V.D's on improving your drive and he talked endlessly about how his concentration was not to be diverted from his game; and so, Tanya felt quite at liberty once again, to indulge her pleasant pastime of sampling Italian marble sculptures. Funnily enough a certain Italian marble mason had returned on a brief but friendly visit.

She sat with Julia and Tracey eating *Rigatoni and Basila Pomodoro e Melenzane* and drinking iced water (Ella's dietary recommendations were being strictly adhered to) Tanya laughingly told them about Marks' inquisitive enquiries over Ella and her golf. She also told them that she would be going to watch a few of the holes, especially the eighteenth, but she might unfortunately have to take a little time out to practise a few master strokes of her own with a master craftsman to guide and aid her!

Tracey seemed a completely different woman, poised, serenely confident, chic and classy. She felt, she had, in the past six months grown up. A woman of the world; in charge of her own destiny and for the first time in her life; thoroughly enjoying herself.

She and Ella had taken to the golf course with skill and determination. They had of course their own private agendas, Tracey to prove to herself she was a competent and confident lady golfer and being confident well able to enter the business world of wine. Ella's agenda was quite different; she knew she was well capable of pulling power. Both her figure and her golf were eye catching, outstanding; supremely aware of this she positively oozed confidence on Whittley Greens Golf course, and Giles, Oh! Poor Giles, she couldn't wait to watch him flounder at the captains day dinner and the annual awards.

Todd had told her how many of the guys had formed a sort of fan club, how they'd even taken bets on the mixed doubles comp, and what's more how many of them couldn't understand why Giles spent so much time at the golf club? When he'd got such a hot raunchy woman at home. Ah! Me! Todd had smiled happily when he told her that!

Julia listened with quiet pleasure. She hadn't felt as neglected of late, as Tanya had, and over the past few months she had refound something of the old feelings she had for James. He had genuinely tried to be more expressive and to involve her more in his life; he had tried to be more emotionally demonstrative and less reserved. Playing golf with Norma had made him more caring, Norma had made him more aware of Julia's sensitive artistic nature and empathy; Julia's strong support and sympathy had given Norma the courage to go on after Rodney's death, James felt rather proud of his wife!

Julia had found a soul mate in Antonio Ullivari, but their love was of a purely artistic nature, he was too much of a sensitive gentleman to risk their friendship on physical passion, he didn't mind flirting, as they had done when they first met, but now friendship and compassion was what they shared, that and an artist's studio.

Julia told Tracey and Tanya that she would, for Norma's sake, follow the competition and attend the evening dinner and awards, she would sit with Mr Poncepé, Gio and Toni and she would clap and cheer for Norma and James.

Tracey informed them both that her dad was, as he put it, escorting the honourable lady captain, Karen McNaulty Q.C. round the course, and he'd be attending to her needs and listening with baited breath to her wise speech at the dinner. He was completely bowled over by the lady, she was so far above him intellectually and physically but then again, he was financially and emotionally Irish; the best man around and he'd give the lady the best *craic* she'd ever have!

And so they played, on a very bright sunny day in late July. James and Norma were one of the first pairs out. James ever the gentleman insisted that Norma drove off the tee first. Norma tried her very best to drive her ball a long way and to keep it on the fairway she smiled embarrassingly at James and said "Rodney always ended up searching in the rough for me!"

James raised his eyebrows and said "Norma! I don't want to know about your amorous adventures!" and Norma subsided into a fit of giggles. They continued round the course in a pleasant, gentle good humoured vain, and the thought of competing never entered their head; they just enjoyed the game.

Julia collected Mr Poncepé at about 11.30 and arrived at Whittley Green as James and Norma arrived on the fourteenth green. Toni and Gio would come later after they had prepared the restaurants lunchtime menu. Mr Poncepé had organized cover for the shops by his good friend Les Parker, a salt of the earth allotment grower and amateur wine making enthusiast who'd do anything for a bottle of Barolo Reservee and a large lump of Lancashire Tasty. Carlo was genuinely looking forward to watching the ladies play in the competition, especially Norma and Tracey.

He walked towards the fifteenth tee with Julia at his side. The old man had a smile of sweet contentment on his face, as he turned to Julia saying "You know I'm very happy now …you ladies have changed my life and Gio's. I can face my twilight years with contentment and Norma by my side. You don't think that's wrong do you?" Julia kissed Mr Poncepé on his bald head very lightly (she was taller than him) and laughing she gently said "Carlo! You are the kindest gentlest of men. You and Norma deserve each other; you both have loved and lost, so there's no shame in seeking and finding comfort and friendship in the warmth of each other." "You don't think people will talk then? Or be shocked?" Carlo looked at Julia with a sad enquiring gaze, and Julia laughed again at this gentle old man   "Oh! Carlo does it matter….let them talk! If you've found comfort and contentment in each other, we ladies are all really, really pleased for you; now let's watch Norma tee off!"

Julia turned towards the club house, in time to see Mark Barcroft and Ella Smythe- Dawson going to the first tee. Ella looked absolutely gorgeous in the sexiest golf outfit Whittley Green or any golf course had ever seen, it was baby pink and black Lycra. It fitted perfectly where it should and it moved beautifully with her body, especially her curvaceous rounded cheeks, which she wriggled sassily when she addressed the ball. Mark ogled her stance and her figure; he drooled and melted like putty in her hands. He'd lost his concentration and the game had hardly started, he couldn't care less about the bloody golf ball, with boobs and a backside like that who needed to keep their eye on the ball! The ball however, Ella's ball, was very near to the green and Mark realized he was partnering a really fine golfer, one who would

125

make his own swing look rather inferior and his game rather amateurish.

Ella was in her element, confident, sexy and admired, she was playing to an audience of Whittley Green admirers, and amongst them was Tanya Barcroft. She followed the game for the first seven holes, clapping at some of the finer shots, but by the time she had reached the seventh she excused herself from the party saying she had urgent business with a free mason,(well it was with a mason, and she felt the urgency of a meeting! God golf was so utterly boring!)

At 1.30 Tracey Doupe and Giles Smythe- Dawson entered the competition. Giles had been told how fantastically well his wife was playing, and he smiled sheepishly as some of the club members said how they envied him. He didn't quite understand all their remarks about her attire and the way she addressed the ball, and how they'd like to be addressed in the same way! Poor Giles, he was blind to his wife's very obvious talents and accomplishments.

He was however very pleased at the sight of his lady partner. Tracey looked professionally chic, and if golf attire could look sophisticated, this was about as near as it would get, and the outfit echoed the colour of her violet blue eyes and enhanced her delicate complexion. She was a beautiful English rose who was about to show Giles Smythe-Dawson that women could play golf as well as most men and better than some! Todd had trained Whittley Greens gorgeous golfing girls very well and he and half the young male members of Whittley Green were enjoying their golfing display with obvious delight.

Karen McNaulty and Nick joined the last few players out. Nick walked by Karen like a large friendly lap dog, eager to please, yet desperate to play and obey. Ms McNaulty gave him gentle words of encouragement and praise; he lapped them up with adoration and admiration written all over his face. The game was wonderful and the golf wasn't bad either.

As James and Norma finished on the 18th, Gio and Toni joined Mr Poncepé and Julia to clap them in. Norma was rosy pink with pleasure, embarrassment and slight sunburn, she hadn't realised how hot and exposed they'd been on the course. "Oh let's have a nice cup of tea! And some of those lovely sandwiches the club has put out, and let's all have a sit down, my feet are killing me!"

Gio took Norma's hand and whispered softly "Norma—I'm sorry Toni and I can't stay long, we're very busy at Penguino's, lots of reservations for this evening and we have so much to do! I was wondering Norma if it's alright with you, Toni she works so hard, standing so long; and as Papa's here with you; can he take you back home, and stay? Then Toni doesn't have to drive all the way back from Clitheroe—She can stay with me...Please say yes!"

There was a long pause of embarrassing anticipation from Toni and Gio. Carlo put his hands up to his cheeks and looked pleadingly at Norma. Norma picked up her tea cup, sipped some tea very slowly, then smiled brightly and said "What a sensible idea, I don't know why you haven't thought of that before!" All of the party sat round the table they sighed visibly, and ate salmon and cucumber sandwiches and sipped tea, knowing that Gio and Toni were about to become lovers for the very first time.

Chapter Twenty five.

The Captain's Dinner Awards Presentation and The Lovers Sublime Consummation.

Mr Poncepé took Norma home to get dressed for the Captains dinner and awards, she didn't expect to be awarded anything, but the pleasure of all her friends company was enough for her, that, and the knowledge that Toni and Gio were about to become one was truly icing on the cake. She sighed with pleasure and gave Carlos hand a very hard affectionate squeeze. Carlo took a large magnum of champagne in the car, he would ask if he could share it with the ladies at the dinner, his joy was as obvious as Norma's and they wanted to share it with the Ladies Italian Society.

Ella and Giles Smythe-Dawson would be seated at the Captains top table as would Karen McNaulty and Nick Murphy; she was the lady captain and he, her escort for the evening. Giles was the vice-captain and forthcoming captain and Ella his good lady wife. The retiring captain sat with his very large and very grumpy wife. She was looking daggers at Ella, perhaps because Ella's cocktail dress had a very plunging neckline that gave her cleavage an eye-catching exposure and the dress was a rather shiny luminous lime green as well! The colour showed off Ella's beautiful tan and her chocolate brown cascading locks to their best advantage; yes she was truly gorgeous, and Giles bless him! Hadn't a clue that nearly every man in the room envied him, and not because he was going to be Whittley Greens' next captain!

Tanya sat with Mark at Norma and James table along with Carlo, Tracey and Julia, they all looked chic and sophisticated in their almost regimental black or navy blue cocktail dresses, all save Norma, Norma couldn't look sophisticated to save her life, she just looked lovely, as dumpy

128

cuddly cosy as she always looked, but there was a happy and excited radiance about her face that expressed her desire to tell Tracey, Tanya and Mark their wonderful news. Mr Poncepé placed the magnum of champagne in an ice bucket next to him. He looked at them all and laughing said "Please a little later I want you all to have champagne, we have a special toast Yes?" and he and Norma just burst into good humoured giggles. Tanya looked almost relieved, at least she wouldn't have to listen to endless descriptions of golf shots all evening, and she liked champagne even if it was only just one glass. She smiled wanly at Julia, and tried not to look bored! She really couldn't stand bloody golf, especially when Mark talked incessantly about it.

James held Julia's hand and asked if she had enjoyed the afternoon, and to his surprise Julia said she had, mainly because she had had Carlo's and Gio's life history and all his hopes for Gio. And Norma couldn't contain their secret any longer and she blurted out in excited gasps "Oh! It's wonderful really, Gio told us in the club house after our game James! He's going to marry Toni!... That's why we've brought the champagne. It's a shame Gio and Toni aren't here to have some, but they've got a more important thing to do tonight!"

James shook his head, he couldn't get over how Norma never realized her words could have a vastly different meaning, she was a truly sweet innocent old dear, who often made double entendres.

The top table gave out their speeches, and Giles, with his long held ambition finally coming to fruition beamed with euphoric pleasure. He accepted the role of golf captain and its considerable expenses. He thanked the retiring captain for his diligence and hard work, and hoped that he would take up the challenging role as capably as his predecessor.

It was a very chummy   time and toasts all round, but then it was the ceremony of handing out the trophies and awards of the golf club. The retiring captain called upon the retiring lady captain Ms McNaulty to give the presentation.

Ms McNaulty looked serenely round the room, put on her gold rimmed spectacles and began to read her opening speech. She was proud to be awarding the trophies for the mixed doubles, but first she had to pay a special tribute to her escort of the day Mr Nicholas Murphy. He had been a true gentleman of golf; his attendance to her needs had been without fault. She had judged him and not found him wanting! And as she was about to take her place on the bench of Lincolns Inn, she felt quite sure of her judgement. She presented an astonished Nick Murphy with a small trophy inscribed with the words "Many thanks for escorting the lady captain Judge McNaulty July 2011."

Tracey and all the ladies of the Italian Appreciation Society clapped, Norma even cheered. Gosh! Their friend and lady captain was about to become a judge, they really had got a lot to celebrate; they were really moving up in the world. Tracey could see her father was really enjoying being part of the group, and that made her realize just how much she had missed his fatherly input over the years.

Karen McNaulty tapped the table with her spoon, and informed everyone that it was the moment to reveal the winning pair of the mixed doubles compertition.She smiled and raising her glass she asked Mark Barcroft and his very able golfing partner Ella Smythe-Dawson to come forward and receive the trophy as the winners of Whittley Green mixed doubles competition.

Mark flushed with success, and a lot of whisky chases, walked clumsily to the stand, everyone politely clapped, but as Ella rose to take to the stand the applause became deafening, there were wolf whistles and cheers. Ella rose to the occasion beautifully her lime green mock snake skin dress shimmered and slid round her supple curves, she shook her cascading chestnut brown hair and threw back her head and walked almost seductively to the stand, and the cheering got even louder.

Mark ogled her with lecherous eyes and a supercilious grin, he slurred "Well, I never thought I'd be beaten by a woman, but you're the best thing Whittley Green golf course has got" and he slid his arm around Ella's curvaceous waist. Ella surmised there was more lecherous behaviour to come and went into feminine attack mode. She put her head charmingly and coquettishly to one side, raised a wicked eyebrow, and removing Marks already creeping hand, she huskily but audibly said "Down boy, down, you haven't got what it takes to beat the best thing Whittley Green golf course trained!" Ella smiled sweetly at him and gently pushed him away; Ella took the trophy from Karen McNaulty and raised it up for everyone to see, a triumphant dental floss smile on her face.

"I'd like to thank my husband Giles(she blew him a kiss) darling!thankyou so much for being so patient with me, you hadn't got an inkling about and not a clue about my secret golf lessons, I knew I'd surprise you! It was Giles ambition to be captain of this golf course! And it became my ambition to be the best lady golfer I could be! I do hope I've fulfilled my full potential!"

With that Ella walked Mark and the golf trophy slowly and triumphantly back to Norma's table, where Norma and Mr Poncepé were waiting to pop their champagne. The Whittley Green men cheered and clapped, Whittley Green had certainly never before seen a lady golfer of such calibre, and Todd Horner Mann Jr, the club professional, knew Mrs Smythe-Dawsons potential was definitely on the up, almost at its peak!

"Oh! Ella you look absolutely gorgeous, wonderful, like a movie star! So glamorous!"

Norma was standing up and clapping and smiling at Ella, and as Ella lent forward to give her a friendly kiss Norma gasped and couldn't help saying "Oh! Ella my dear you look as though you've been poured into that durex dress!"

Everyone round the table and near it guffawed at Norma's exclamation, but not Ella. She threw back her head and laughed a rather sexy throaty laugh, and said quite loud enough for all to hear "No Norma I hope I'm going to be pawed in my Lurex dress later this evening!"

The ladies all guessed what Ella meant and Tracey patiently explained to Norma, who of course whooped with embarrassment at what she had said, she wiped away a tear of amusement from her eye and said "Oh! Ella you are naughty… but oh! So nice. I do so love you girls, you've made my boring ordinary old life really bearable, you and Mr P. especially after my poor Rodney's passing, but do you know I think he'd love this evening!" Ella doubted that, it was rather too hasty for Rodney's dour ways and much, much too exciting.

Tracey's mobile rang and she listened to it as the others sipped the champagne, she beamed around them and put the phone down. "Well that was Antonio, calling to tell you Gio and Toni have just announced their engagement, and Toni has asked Antonio if they can be married in the Ullivari Gallery. Toni and Gio have gone home to celebrate and consummate their forth coming nuptials. I gather Gio was quite high on Barolo, but desperately happy to be taken home by Toni!"

Carlo Poncepé stood up and raised his champagne glass "I give you a toast my dear friends;Iam so happy! Please, I ask you to join with me. Here's to my son Giovanni and to his wonderful bride to be Toni Burghini, soon to be Mrs Poncepé!" Every one of the ladies of the Italian Art and Cultural Appreciation Society raised their glasses and joined in the toast, even if Ella only drank mineral water and Tanya had just the one glass of champagne.

Chapter Twenty six.

The Proposal and after the preparation of a wedding in the Ullivari Gallery.

Toni held Gio's hand and lead him to their little mini, he was laughing and trembling at the same time. Everyone knew they were going to be married, and everyone knew they were going home together, and that Carlo wouldn't be there to chaperone his gentle innocent virginal son.

Gio turned to Toni and raised her hand to his lips, he kissed her finger tips and placed one into his mouth and gently nibbled it.Toni laughingly pulled him close to her body, kissing him full on the lips and pushing her tongue into his mouth whilst placing his sensitive fingers round her already erect rosy pink nipples." Oh! God! Oh! Toni! Please help me… my whole body's on fire, I don't know what you do to me but I want it so much!" And Toni laughed again and teasingly whispered in his ear "Oh! Gio! You'll have to wait till we get home and then I'll show you! Help you! Guide you! Ok?" She teased him stroking his beautiful hair, his neck, his face and he allowed her to guide him into the car.

She drove as quickly as the darkness would allow Gio kept telling her how much he wanted her, how he wanted to feel her strong warm body next to his, and Toni placed her warm moist hand onto the bare skin of his chest and Gio moaned in an exquisite agony of anticipation. "Later, darling let's get home first!" whispered Toni.

They laughed as the car came to a halt outside the large Victorian three storey villa. Toni helped Gio out of the car and he leaned on her shoulder, he was a little intoxicated with Barolo and heady with love. He was however still very sensitively aware of what was about to happen, and as he unlocked the front door of his home he turned towards Toni, he put his hand under her scarred chin and raised her head, feeling for her lips he tenderly kissed her and said "Toni, before we go any further I want you to know… I love you (here he paused for a moment) I love every inch of you and that includes what is growing in you, because it's part of you, and I want it to be part of me! I want it to be mine! I want it to have my name, and I want no-one to know it's not mine. Is that right with you?"

"Oh Gio! you are the best of men, I promise we will have many babies, a houseful of children! All yours, but first I have to give you your manhood!" Toni kissed him on his cheek as she slowly started guiding Gio up the staircase in the dark. Gio being blind and in his own home needed no guidance, but he encouraged Toni all the same to put her arm around his waist, he leaned towards her as he opened his bedroom door, he didn't turn on the light saying "I don't need the light Toni, do you?" and Toni softly laughed crooning, the lights went out! Papa went out and I was left all alone with you! Gio it's much more fun, feeling your way in the dark, come closer and let me find you!" There was a long silence after that, and then much sighing and gasped breathing, and the soft swishing sound of clothing falling gently to the floor.

The gentle flop of Gio as he was pushed back onto his extra-large king size bed was the last sound, from that moment there was no sound for some time, then only the sound of Gio's ecstatic sighs as Toni guided his Cupids arrow into her very core, till the final orgasmic moment when Gio's manhood flooded over Toni and Gio shouted "Oh! Yes! Yes! God yes! Oh! God yes!"

This sublime moment of ecstasy occurred at the very same moment as Ella exclaimed she hoped to be pawed in her rather seductive lime green Lurex mock snake skin dress. So the ladies of the Italian Appreciation Society ended the Whittley Green Golf Awards evening on a very ecstatic high. All senses being fulfilled, all potentials met, and revenge if not quite complete, at least very very sweet.

Julia took James and Mark home, they were both quite intoxicated with golf, champagne and a considerable number of whisky chasers; Julia was happy to relieve Tanya of her wifely duty as Tanya was going to return with Tracey to Penguinos, ostensibly to discuss wedding plans, but more likely marble alter tables and their sensuous smooth surface.

It would be a civil wedding in the Ullivari Gallery, the registration of the marriage would be signed on the very same alter table Tanya was seduced on; but this would be a very public ceremony, watched over by all the ladies of the Italian Appreciation Society, a few errant golfers and lots of romantic Italian waiters and wine lovers, yes, it was going to be a very Italian affair.

Vittorio Tartaglioni had returned to Lancashire and was enjoying a late supper with Antonio Ullivari when Tanya and Tracey arrived. The restaurant was closing, but the kitchen was still warm and the waiters just leaving. Vittorio rose from the supper and greeted Tanya lifting her in a bear hug embrace. "So my little temptress has returned to tease me!" Tanya grinned and asked if there was any *Gamberoni Provinciale* around, and Vittorio answered "No but you can share my plate if you want. It's not *Gamberoni* but the pasta is good and I'll even feed it to you; Italian style!" He pulled her down to sit closely next to him. Tracey looked at Antonio and gave him a gentle knowing nod.

While Tanya and Vittorio played eat the spaghetti Italian style (one string between two mouths) Antonio and Tracey discussed the nuptial arrangements of Toni and Gio. It would be very simple but beautiful, full of delights to the senses especially those of touch, taste and smell this was for Gio, but above all else it would be very Italian.

Antonio looked deep into Tracey's violet-blue eyes, as she described this idea to him. He was beginning to more than admire this woman; she was very like Julia in many ways, sensitive, caring and fully aware of others feelings. He wanted her to know that he admired her greatly especially her sensitive nature. He told her he thought the idea was excellent, he would make all the arrangements for the civil wedding, but could she organize the sensuous parts. Tracey looked back into Antonio's dark longing eyes and fluttering her own lashes and blushing said "I'd like that very much, but I think we need to discuss that in more detail, don't you!" Antonio ever the gentleman raised her hand to his lips and kissed it. "I think that's an excellent idea, we'll talk about it in my apartment." The two of them rose from the table, leaving Tanya and Vittorio engrossed in each other, they walked hand in hand to the black and gold door to Antonio's beautiful Italian apartment to make nuptial arrangements amongst other things.

Chapter Twenty seven.

The Wedding, the Reception and After the Dinner Some Confessions and Revelations.

On the last day of September, in bright autumn sunshine Giovanni Poncepé and Toni Burghini walked hand in hand through the narrow drive to Penguino's restaurant and the Ullivari Gallery. They entered it gliding through the magnificent replicas of renaissance sculptures and paintings. Tracey had arranged for all the highly scented beautiful flower arrangements to be placed in between the alcoves and statues. The air was filled with the heavy scent of lilies, jasmine and roses. The lighting was romantically subdued and the atmosphere in the gallery was invitingly warm and cosy, in fact everything that could delight the senses was in the room, warmth, perfume and the sound of sweet voices singing softly in the background.

All the ladies of the Italian Appreciation Society were there dressed in their finery. Their men folk James, Mark and Giles dressed in smart casual wear (Mark and Giles looked remarkably like they were going to the golf club.)The Italians as ever, Sauvé, sophisticated and yet so fashionable, stood near the statue of David, they had a large magnum of champagne on ice, ready for the exact moment the marriage certificate was signed.

Ella looked absolutely gorgeous, as did Tracey, both these ladies were getting a reputation in the area for being both astute business women and fashion gurus, and to this end they had started yet another business venture, fashionable golfing attire for the discerning lady golfer. Tracey was the financial and business partner and Ella the designer and advertising director; the ladies enjoyed each other's company and liked bouncing ideas off each other, as well as sharing golf lessons with Todd. The pair looked chic and sophisticated without being over the top, they had that art of understated class and it showed.

Julia and Tanya floated in to the gallery in swishy silk outfits, beautifully tailored yet flowing and floaty in subdued pastel shades. Neither wore a hat, it wasn't that sort of wedding.

Last to arrive before the entrance of Gio and Toni, was Norma on the arm of Carlo. They both looked elderly but truly happy, blissful contentment written all over them. Norma in powder blue with matching hat, gloves, handbag and shoes, she looked very like the queen mother. Carlo looked like the cat that'd got all the cream, all smiles and nods to everyone. His hopes and dreams for Gio were about to be fulfilled, he knew that with Toni, he would have a happy and full life; and Carlo felt Toni would be able to blossom into the gentle feminine woman she really was with Gio by her side. She would always be the master chef but now she'd no longer have the bitter hatred for men that could have consumed her, Gios love and innocence had won her.

Gio and Toni arrived; both wore the palest blue grey velvet. Gio had a soft velvet jacket, a dove grey silk shirt and grey suede trousers; he had used his fine sense of touch in the choice of fabrics. Toni had echoed the materials in her flowing silk dress and velvet cloak. She carried no flowers but held Gios hand in both of hers, she looked radiantly happy and Gio told her she was, in his eyes, the most beautiful woman in the world, he could smell her hair and feel it on his cheek, and he could feel her trembling tingling heart beating through her warm hands, their joy was there for all to see.

A simple civil ceremony took place and Antonio Ullivari translated it to Gio and Toni as it took place. Toni signed the marriage certificate as did Gio, he had been practising his signature with Toni's help and, on this day, he wrote his name. As the registrar handed the marriage certificate over to Gio, Gio gave Toni a thin gold ring, it had been his mothers, and inscribed on the inner side it read Carlo and Georgina love forever. On the outer edge Gio had had inscribed Gio and Toni love forever.

Champagne, canapés and anti-pasta started the wedding feast, laughter and congratulations followed. Carlo Poncepé gave flutes of champagne to everyone. He insisted the entire wedding congregation raise their glasses to toast the marriage of his son Gio and Norma's girl Toni.

The ladies of the Italian cultural Appreciation Society gathered round Toni and Gio and embraced them with congratulations, a few photos were taken, but as Gio would never see them and Toni didn't like her picture taken, little time was spent in posing. It was time to spend doing what Italians love doing, eating, drinking and wooing. Antonio invited his guests to an Italian wedding feast in the restaurant.

Julia and Tanya sat with James and Mark, Ella with Giles, Karen McNaulty came for the ceremony only, she was attending a Bench meeting in London and had to travel down in the evening, but she wanted to see Toni's wedding, and to know that Toni had for all her torture, found love and fulfilment. Norma and Carlo sat with Toni and Gio, and Tracey and Antonio Ullivari at the large marble table. Vittorio was with all the waiters and wine lovers; he was enjoying the wine and good food in the traditional sense of true Italian spirit. He raised his glass to Tanya though, when the first main course was brought to the tables. Antonio Ullivari raised his voice saying "Ladies and gentlemen for the wedding feast I give you Aphrodite's temptingly seductive aphrodisiac dish *Gamberoni Provinciale!*"

Julia and Tanya looked at each other and grinned, Julia told James this was her favourite Italian dish, it awakened her sense of touch, taste and smell, and she showed him how to eat it the Italian way. Tanya watched as James and Julia happily tucked into the dish. Mark just pushed the king prawns round his plate saying he didn't like having to fiddle and fafe about with skin and heads and all that. Tanya shook her head, Mark was being the spoilt little brat, and she knew he was getting ready to leave the table to go and play; how long would he last at the feast? It was an Italian wedding and there would be course after course of really good and tasty food.

Maiale Arrosto (roast pig)

Porchetta (roast suckling pig)

Arrosto Misto (mixed roast)

These dishes were brought to the tables with side dishes of *Carciofi*, *Radicchio* and *Pisilli*.The Italians loved their food and enjoyed it with a gusto that was catching to everyone, except Mark and Giles, they lasted through the *Porchetta*, Mark saying he'd rather have a pork chop and chips. Tanya knew it was time for him to remove himself, before he insulted the hosts of this wonderful feast. She turned to him and quite deliberately, witheringly said "I'm sure you and Giles would far rather be at the golf club, and I know your clubs are in the boot—so why don't you just go- no one will miss you!" Mark being the silly selfish little boy he was grinned from ear to ear. He looked over to Giles who seemed just as relieved and then he turned to James saying "Are you game for a knock eh! Jimmy?"

James was not really game for a knock, but Julia took him to one side and said "It's alright James; they need you to take them and be the big brother. I think Giles has had a little too much champagne and I know Mark has. I'll get a taxi home with Tanya, don't worry you know I'll come home safe and sound to you." She kissed him on his smooth forehead. James looked a little sheepish and guilty, he felt he was letting Julia down, but as she'd given him her blessing, he went to Carlo and Antonio and gave them his thanks and asked if they'd excuse the golfers as they'd a place on the team to fulfil. Giles and Mark were like two little school boys let out of school early. They checked that their clubs were all there in the boot and happily waved bye to the ladies. Tanya and Ella didn't even miss them going, their present company was much more exciting.

The *dolci* came, sweet ice cream, sorbets, an assortment of *tortas* and *tiramisu* with sweet wines, and just when Julia thought they couldn't possibly manage anymore and the coffee was being poured Carlo Poncepé rose and asked for every ones attention. He raised his glass of *Barolo Reservee* and said "ladies and gentlemen, Norma has enjoyed today so much as I have, but she wanted to bring something special for the feast, so we have many cheese boards for you all to try and some *Barolo* to accompany it. But Norma she has a very special surprise, can you bring it in?" Two waiters wheeled in a covered trolley from the kitchen, and on it was a five tiered ornate wedding cake. Everyone cheered and clapped. After Toni and Gio cut it, the cake was taken away to be cut and served in special little boxes to each guest.

The afternoon was moving fast into the evening and the guests were gathering into various comfortable groups. Toni and Gio were off for a short week-end break at a secret location somewhere in the lakes. Carlo and Norma were eating cheese and sipping *Barolo*, with a contented look on their faces.

Ella was sitting very happily in the middle of a group of Italian designers and business men, flirting madly but not dangerously. Tracey was deep in conversation with Antonio Ullivari and Tanya was teasingly flirting with Vittorio, she turned and looked at Julia. Julia sat very still, sipping her coffee; she had a dreamy smile as she looked wistfully over the restaurant.

Tanya moved over to Julia and sat next to her, she nudged her arm saying "Tell me what you're day dreaming or reminiscing about?" Tanya raised a wicked eyebrow and gave a questioning look at Julia, and Julia chuckled. "Yes, I was just thinking, it's been an eventful journey since that night in February, when we dared ourselves to come here. We so wanted to escape from boredom, and we needed revenge for being left on the shelf as it were, while the men had all the pleasure of their favourite pass time!"

"Oh! God yes! I got my revenge alright, in fact I'm still reaping it. You know I do so love Italian marble! But I need the finer points of it to be highlighted for me, by a master mason!" Tanya looked over at Vittorio; he was enjoying Ella's splendid hips and breasts. "The pleasure he gets from ogling women is beyond belief, he says it's his favourite pastime, but he's never met a woman as wickedly exciting as me, and I'm the best lady he's ever fucked!" Julia slurped her coffee as she laughed out "Tanya! I told you that night, it's your revenge, I didn't want to know, but I guessed you had a rather erotic time behind the tapestry. We allowed ourselves to be seduced that night, in fact Tanya, you invited it!"

"Oh I got what I deserved! And I wanted it, I still do. Vittorio treats me like a voluptuous Goddess, he loves every inch of me, and what's more he tells me I'm worth it! I get my pleasure my way, Vittorio gets his, and Mark gets his pleasure the golf way. We're all happy, nobody gets hurt and we keep our lives separate, besides Mark gave up sex years ago. Ella says Giles doesn't have any interest in sex as well, it must be a golf thing!"

Julia grinned, she knew Tanya was fishing; she wanted to know if Julia was still as bored with James as she was with Mark. "Well! Are you going to tell me, or must I ask?" Tanya turned Julia to face her and very quietly asked "Are you and James back to being happy bed fellows?" Julia looked over the rim of her coffee cup and grinned "Well we nearly lost it for a while back in February, in fact we were like ships that passed in the night, I didn't seem to need James and I thought he didn't need me. I'd got the Italian society and he'd got the golf; but it was Rodney's death that brought us to our senses, and James even admitted he needed me, wanted me, we've been trying to be more aware of each other's needs since then."

"So you don't mind if Antonio Ullivari gets really pally with Tracey, I see, you're not a golf widow anymore, and you don't need any revenge. But you won't tell James about my confessions will you? You'll keep it a secret." Tanya knew that Julia would never reveal what happened between Vittorio and her, but she was still itching to find out what Julia and Antonio had got up to that first night at Penguino's.

"I thought you'd go the whole hog with Antonio, especially after all that erotic talk about aphrodisiac *Gamberoni*, and the graphically seductive scene you two got up to eating it the sensuous Italian way!" Tanya paused and waited and looked pleadingly at Julia. Julia just smiled and carried on drinking her coffee. "Well did you or didn't you? Where did you two go, while Vittorio showed me his marble masterpiece?" Tanya was laughing now quizzing Julia, she was desperate to know "Oh come on Julia, you can tell me, I promise I won't be shocked and I'll never tell?"

"Oh! You really want to know don't you...Well I won't tell you… but if you come with me I'll show you!" Julia put down her coffee and stood up; she waved to Antonio and pointed to the black and gold doors. He nodded his head and continued talking with Tracey. "Come on Tanya…this is where we went after you and Vittorio disappeared behind the tapestry!"

Julia opened the large doors for Tanya and revealed a sweeping staircase with yet another door at the top. "Oh this gets more and more exciting … is it a sexy, sensual French boudoir?" asked Tanya. Julia just smiled and led the way to the door. It was a dimly lit, yet invitingly warm staircase, and the ladies climbed slowly to the top. Julia opened her neat little clutch bag and produced an ornate key. She turned the lock and the door quietly opened to reveal a room shrouded in darkness. The ladies walked in and Julia switched the lights on. In the glaring artificial light, Tanya turned round and looked at a large artist's studio.

There were two easels facing towards a platform with drapes hanging from a pillar. Julia stood by a long trestle table that had pallets, brushes and paints on, she grinned at Tanya. "Antonio's working on a new painting, and I've been asked to work on a commission for a fitness emporium in Thirsk." "Oh!" said Tanya, she looked a little disappointed, but Julia nodded her head and pointed at the far wall behind Tanya.

Tanya turned her, glance towards the wall and gasped.

There was a large almost life sized painting hanging on the wall. It was monochrome, but that only added to its overwhelming masculine power. It was a portrait of a man, strong tall and erect. His torso and limbs turning and swivelled, were painted with powerful brush strokes that conveyed strength in its very nakedness. His body expressed pulsating, sensuous sexuality just about to explode. But it was not the body that compelled the viewer to look, no, it was the man's face as it turned to stare out from the painting. The eyes so spirited, piercing and shamelessly leaping out, they are begging, pleading with desire, and they are unmistakeably the eyes of Antonio Ullivari.

Tanya, wide eyed and open mouthed gasped. "Wow! You've certainly captured him!"

She looked at Julia in admiration, but Julia pointed in the direction of the opposite wall, so Tanya's attention moved to yet another life sized portrait.

It was the portrait of an unforgettably beautiful woman lying unashamedly naked on a billowing downy couch. Her shoulders and breasts raised and arched in a sensual sexual orgasm. Her whole body painted as if blushing and rosy pink with pleasure, the plump skin seemingly ripe at the height of orgasmic fulfilment.

The face of the lady expresses pure sexual pleasure, her mouth half open in a sigh of ecstatic joy and her eyes half closed in ecstasy. Her face graphically expressing sexual consummation of a sublime nature, and the face of the lady was unmistakeably Julia Halifax.

"You did! Didn't you?" exclaimed Tanya "Bloody hell! The pair of you painted each other afterwards! Julia that is absolutely mind blowing! Did you both paint at the same time?" Julia laughed and walked up to the painting of Antonio, she stroked the edge of it lovingly, and said "It took three months to paint, and yes! We started them that first night. But I'll leave it up to you to decipher the paintings and decide what we did or didn't do!" Tanya was staring at the portrait of the reclining nude and shaking her head in disbelief, turning to Julia she asked "Well, I think you got your revenge, but was it bitter sweet?"

"Ah! Ha" said Julia "it's all in the eye of the beholder! But let's put it this way, these portraits are not for public viewing. They are for a purely personal and very private fulfilment, and I think I've found my full potential and reaped my Golf widow's revenge!"

Tanya put her arm round her friends shoulder, she held a key ring in her other hand, it was a marble key ring, small but exquisitely carved, and it was a perfect phallic symbol. "I think we both got our revenge. Come on I'll drive home this time!"

THE END.

288882BV00010B/10/P
BV0W011427270412
Printed in the USA
CPSIA information can be obtained at www.ICGtesting.com